N

A Cyborg S.........

. . . .

By Naomi Lucas

Cover Art by Cameron Kamenicky
Editing by Lindsay York at LY Publishing Services
Editing by Tiffany Freund

• • • •

Stranded in the Stars
Last Call
Collector of Souls
Star Navigator
Larik (Coming Fall 2018)

Cyborg Shifters
Wild Blood
Storm Surge
Shark Bite
Mutt
Ashes and Metal (Coming Spring 2018)

Valos of Sonhadra
Radiant (Coming February 2018)

Chapter One

· · · ·

C lara sat in her land-flyer at a loss for words. She didn't know if it was karma she was facing or just downright, scum-covered, bad-fucking-luck.

The hum of her vehicle, shaky and rough, only reminded her of all the mistakes she had made, and the past life she was fleeing.

She pressed her finger into the scanner and shifted the vehicle into neutral with a sigh. A chime sounded from the speakers right as the first beads of sweat glistened above her brow, and a name appeared over her windshield, transparent in its neutral, projected blue. She had to squint to read it.

Marsha Tannett. Clara's contact from the police department in her hometown. She accepted the call.

"Hi, this is Clara speaking..."

"Hey, Clara, it's Marsha from the Pecos PD. We have an update for you, ma'am, but can you verify your full name and address?"

"Clara A. Warren, and I... no longer have an address." She had an address yesterday, a musty rented out motel room, but no longer. Staying in one place for too long was dangerous.

She realized long ago that her enemy would find her wherever she went, and even verifying her personal information via a secure line was still taking a risk. Her hands flexed in her lap.

"What about your date of birth?"

"11 05 2854." She rubbed her sweaty palms over her pants.

"One moment, please," Marsha's voice tuned out.

Clara looked around her, taking in the dry beige desert. Nothing caught her interest, but it had become a habit to check over her shoulder every few minutes, ever since Santino had been released from prison. Everything was dust, dead, irradiated by the unhindered rays of the sun. There was no life, no movement, nothing. It didn't make her feel better, knowing she was the only living being amongst the sterility of the desert wastes.

The line tuned back in. "Sorry Ms. Warren, always have to check. About that update—"

"Which is?"

"Your ex checked into a halfway house—"

"Where?"

"Outside the Dallas metropolis, Pleasant Grove, ma'am—"

"When?"

Marsha grumbled, "Yesterday morning."

Yesterday morning. Clara took in her surroundings again; the flat fields of powdery dirt and dried husks of vegetation that drank their last drop of water an age past. *Santino could be anywhere by now. Anywhere.*

It was suddenly hard to breathe.

"Are you still there, ma'am?"

"Yes," Clara croaked out as she switched her flyer out of neutral. A soft breeze of conditioned air coursed over her face, chilling the sweat on her skin and making her shiver.

"If you have the funds, we can deploy a protection-model android to guard you."

Clara closed her eyes.

She didn't have the money to afford android security. In fact, she had just enough saved to be on the run for a couple months, well, now that she no longer had a wedding to plan for. Clara glanced down at the white band of skin where her engagement ring used to be and wilted...

She wilted in the middle of the desert where no one would see her. Where, for a brief second, she belonged with the dead, the debris, and the dirt.

Clara was done with men. Done with her sadistic ex and her fiancé who had broken off their engagement—not a week after he discovered the baggage she carried. She was done being hurt, used up, and thrown out. All she wanted out of life was a little security, a family, and to wake up with a smile on her face in the morning.

Am I asking for too much? Is what I want akin to the world?

"Don't bother," she quipped then added, "Thank you for the news." Clara moved to disconnect the call.

"Ms. Warren?"

Her finger hovered. "Yes?"

"Please reach out to us if you need anything."

They disconnected.

Clara picked up her tablet and stared at the screen where she had bookmarked the only option she had left for the future she wanted.

No more men. No more pain. I can have it all. Security, family, and hopefully that morning smile. She brushed her fingers across her stomach, remembering the pain. It had been gone for a long time and she didn't know what she hated more: that the pain was gone and no longer occupied all her thoughts, or that its absence had burgeoned a new, worse pain in her heart.

Clara sighed and put her vehicle back into self-drive. It lifted into the air, sweeping dust around her windshields, temporarily cloaking her shaken heart from the world.

She was going nowhere fast and vastly off-kilter.

The dirt cleared and the desert re-emerged, along with an unsettling feeling that she was being watched. She kissed her fingertips and tapped the roof of her vehicle, praying that she was making the right choice.

The Cyborg breeding facility—the name made her flinch—was set in her GPS. *Bred up, bred once, bred well and good.* Her pamphlet relayed no statistics on success or failure; in fact, the information it held was subpar at best. It was *old*. The paper edges were worn and frayed but she knew it still existed. She knew that much at least.

She had never heard of a Cyborg fathering children and that was fine with her. She wasn't going there to get knocked up by test-tube sperm...

Clara fisted her hand into the loose cloth of her shirt.

If she did get pregnant, fine, it would save her a step, but if she didn't, her next stop would be a fertility center to ply herself with human designer seed.

No more men. She wanted to shout out her window and scream it to the world.

The landscape blurred and her flyer shot forward. The chimes pinned to her dashboard swayed with the continuous blast of air conditioning, their fragmented garnet and crystal stones refracting rainbows over her face.

No one would suspect she was crying. No one would know that she shivered, not from the cold air, but from uncertainty.

I'm running away.

She only hoped that whatever was chasing her would never catch up.

Chapter Two

• • • •

Reid stared out his office window at the flyer sitting at the back of the parking lot. He plucked at his lips with his thumb and pointer finger.

The vehicle had arrived two hours ago, passed through all of the facility's security, and obtained a visitor's pass. The occupant had been fingerprinted, eye-scanned, given contracts to sign, placed in holding while the flyer was checked over, and eventually, after all the trouble it took to gain access to the front door, decided to sit her old metal hulk down and not move.

At first he'd been annoyed, but now he was intrigued.

The visitor's information sat open on his console, a holographic image of a face projected before him. Reid had memorized it—unwillingly—and captured it so it would remain in his head, behind his eyelids, and in his personal hard drives forever until he either died or deleted it.

Clara Anne Warren.

The name simply represented the next woman he'd have to turn away from the program.

She'd be one of many in a long list of hopefuls: infertile couples looking for a fix, women—sometimes men—who wanted to indulge their Cyborg fetish once and for all, single-women homeless and poor looking for a place to stay and get medical care. The last group stabbed at his cold and bloodless metal heart.

Reid wasn't a saint but neither was he callous. Those women always left with a recommendation from him for the nearest medical plaza, where they would be treated and taken care of with their expenses paid for by the facility.

They never came back. They never needed to.

He clasped his hands behind his back, stretching his suit tight over his chest; its restraints cut into his freedom. He was different, not because he was a shifter Cyborg, but because he had a tendency to shift into his beast... and never want to shift back.

Reid checked his watch. Fifteen hundred hours. Clara had still yet to leave her vehicle. The projected image of her face burned a hole into his back.

She was a thirty-one-year-old female, unattached, but made a handful of bad choices in her past. She had an ex who had recently been released from prison, a series of venue cancellations, a disturbing history of medical issues and surgeries, and barely a penny left to her name.

Reid tilted his head. There was movement beyond the glare of the vehicle's windshield. Clara was *just* what he needed: another woman knocking on his door, another pair of sad eyes to turn away.

He sighed, straightened, and peeled out of his blazer, meticulously smoothing any wrinkles and hanging it behind his office door. He loosened his shirt and unbuttoned the first two clasps at his throat before he cracked his neck and stretched out his fingers.

All this he did while refusing to look at the image of the woman on his wall. He wouldn't get distracted by soft curves, plush lips twitched up into a smile he could only describe as coy, and big, thickly framed violet eyes.

Violet eyes the color of a downtown metropolis at happy hour. The color of an Elyrian three sunset, each star blending a different purple into the horizon, violet and bottomless, and powerful enough to bring a man to his knees.

He had never seen the like. But he wasn't a man; he was a Cyborg, and one with a heart encased in steel, frozen by his choice of career. A frozen heart couldn't beat. At least that's what he told himself to get through the day. A pair of unusual eyes meant nothing to him.

He chose to ignore that they were plastered on his wall, and returned to his post by the window, knowing that even if Clara Warren were looking straight at him, she wouldn't be able to see him through the darkly shielded glass.

The land-flyer's door opened. His finger twitched. *You have one more warning, Clara dear. One more.*

She stepped out of the vehicle and he loosened another button on his shirt. Reid squinted, honing in on the woman who slowly emerged from the beat-up metal, his scope tech zooming in. His view of her was unhindered except for the hair that breezed across her face.

He wanted to catch a glimpse of her irises. He told himself it wasn't for their color, or that he cared, but to see if hers were tinged with sadness like the rest.

But her head was bowed low and she'd tugged a pair of sunglasses down her face. She lifted her head as her hair wisped around her cheeks and turned full circle before she faced the facility again, and as she made her way toward him, she kept looking behind her.

Reid trailed her progress. Her skin glistened with a sheen of sweat, and her pulse fluttered like a frightened sparrow.

What're you looking for, Clara? It made him scan the grounds despite already knowing nothing was there.

Her face tilted up and looked directly at his window. He stiffened regardless of the fact that she couldn't see him.

One more warning.

She picked up her pace and continued approaching the facility, the flops of her sandals easily heard through the cement and metal barrier between them. His ears pricked despite his carefully feigned indifference, an indifference and cold demeanor that had taken him years to cultivate. He'd frozen his instincts, burying them so deep into his coding it would take an exceptionally skilled hacker to find them.

Reid loosened his cuffs, turned away, and waited to see if she'd heed his final warning.

• • • •

BEWARE OF DOG

Clara stared at the sign, reading it, and reading it again.

She glanced around her, over the nearly empty parking lot and its steaming asphalt, to the triple-gated fences, along the entrance and exit, but saw no dog, nor any sign that there had ever been one.

She shrugged it off.

She had examined everything within the vicinity of her vehicle, buying her time. Now that she didn't have any more check stops between her and her destination, she no longer had any reason to turn around.

The decision to contract with CBF would have been infinitely easier if it had been taken out of her hands.

Raising her glasses onto her head, she twisted and glared at her car, half expecting to see her sadistic ex leaning up against it, but it sat alone in all its old glory. It hadn't broken down like she'd hoped on the way. Instead, tt betrayed her and forced her to push through her nervousness. The only obstacle between her and the door was the haze of heat that bathed everything in its path.

That and her own cowardice.

Clara adjusted the shoulder strap of her purse, righted her composure, and walked toward the door. It opened as she neared. The sign vanished behind her.

A blast of air hit her dead in the face, making her cringe. Her skin chilled and in one instant she went from being on the verge of heatstroke to being in danger of frostbite. She rubbed her palms up and down the goosebumps on her arms.

She knew two things: that she was being watched, and that the first step through that door would be the step that turned her life around.

Clara took in the empty reception room.

The interior was white with black metal paneling and floor-to-ceiling glass walls to partition the space. There were two painfully white plastic chairs facing a reception desk that was manned by no one. Behind it and throughout the room were screens displaying fertility information interspersed with moving images of exotic alien locales.

She approached the desk, unsettled that the only sound in the air was the slaps of her shoes. Everything gleamed, polished to perfection. It was beautiful and stark and... she was completely out of place. Nothing about the entrance room of the facility elicited comfort.

It was utterly dissimilar to the worn cement and barbed wires of the outside; the swirling dust and the scorching heat, where rain hadn't fallen in over a hundred years.

"Hello?"

Her heart pounded as her question echoed. She looked around, hoping to find an android or another living being rushing to assist her, but it remained silent.

"Hello?" she said louder.

Again, no one answered, but a screen raised from the desk. Clara swallowed as she came upon a questionnaire. There was no tablet to take back to a seat for her to answer in comfort. She straightened her back and refused to be deterred and began answering the dozen or so questions with her fingertip.

Have you had surgery anytime the last twelve months? Specify when and for what purpose. If yes, was the procedure medically necessary, medically advised, elective or cosmetic? She answered each of them with a hint of boredom. She had done it all before, dozens of times over the past ten years or so, ever since Santino hurt her.

But as she continued, the questions became more direct, more personal. Clara shifted on her feet, now relieved that the room remained empty.

Have you had any miscarriages? If so how many?

Have you ever had cybernetic surgery? If so, when was it? And for what purpose?

Is this your first time at a breeding facility? If not, where else have you gone?

Clara frowned and stared at the question. *There are other breeding facilities?*

Are you allergic to sperm?

Have you had sexual relations with an alien?

No. No. No.

Do you have a Cyborg fetish?

Clara stopped. *What the?*

She wasn't sure if what she was feeling was confusion, concern, or both. She wiped her finger on the side of her jeans as if it needed to be cleaned.

Do I have a Cyborg fetish? She had seen Cyborg-inspired porn on occasion, she had even thought that some of the newer companion androids were attractive. Clara's pulse thrummed every time she saw an image of the Cyborg heroes in the tabloids.

But it was because they were men, she told herself. *Who doesn't like good-looking men?* She lifted her finger to answer the question but something moved in her periphery.

Clara froze.

Her limbs locked and her stomach dropped. A huge dog stood five yards away from her. *Not a dog.* She swallowed. A huge mechanical, robot beast, one she had never seen the likes of before. It's head reached her waist, it's metal ears higher still. The dog's mere size suggested that it could tear out her neck with one giant bite.

Nothing about it looked weak. It was menacing. *I could ride its back and it probably wouldn't notice me... My feet wouldn't even touch the ground.*

She wasn't small, standard height maybe, but she liked to describe herself as rounded to perfection in all the right places.

But in comparison to the dog, she felt like a brittle-boned sprite, unable to go outside during a windstorm, now faced with an oversized metal beast because she didn't want to be blown away.

Clara forgot all about the questions. Her gaze met the canine's. Its dark eyes were hard and... *Annoyed?* As if she were in its way. She held its gaze, unwavering, despite her nerves, feeling somehow that she had to establish some sort of dominance, regardless of the fear that coursed through her.

He knows I'm afraid.

"Beware of dog," she whispered to herself.

The canine remained unmoving and showed no aggression toward her. It didn't stop her life from flashing before her, knowing that the robotic creature could rip her to shreds and eat her whole if it chose to do so. She canted her head and the dog canted its head back. The corner of her lips lifted into a weak smile.

She was getting somewhere. Her unease waned.

"Is the sign out front... for you?" Clara put her palms out to show the beast she meant no harm.

She took a slow step toward it. It barked. Her smile lifted further. She continued to approach the dog until she was before it and on her knees. A bead of sweat ran down the side of her face leaving a cold path behind from the frigid room temperature.

"You're not so scary, are you?" She kept her hand out for it to sniff her. And in a moment of intelligence, it leaned forward, pressed its snout into her palm, and then backed up.

"You're not scary at all, no you're not," she cooed. Clara loved dogs, always had and always would. Even one created clearly as a weaponized machine couldn't stop the endearment in her voice.

"What's your name?"

It didn't respond.

"You don't speak?" Clara wondered if it had the intelligence of an android. It still did nothing.

"Can I pet you?"

It barked and its eyes flashed again with dark light. She decided to read that as a *yes*. Clara reached out to rub her fingers against the metal plating below its jaw and when it didn't attack her, she pet its chest between.

"You're like a normal dog, aren't you? I'm a friend, yes I am. Hopefully, I don't have to be wary of you and that that sign outside is for bad people," she continued to coo as her fingers slid across the synthetic padding between its metal plates. "We don't like bad guys, do we? No we don't. I don't like bad guys either. But with a majestic dog like you around, I don't think I'd have to worry about them."

Its eyes kept flickering and she eventually moved away. No one else had arrived and the screen with its questions had vanished. She turned back toward the dog.

"Do you know what I'm supposed to do now?" The dog didn't respond. Clara stepped further away, swallowing, but as she did, the beast turned on its heel and disappeared around the corner and into the facility.

Does he want me to follow it? Him? Her?

She glanced around the quiet space again and shrugged before she trailed after the canine. It was waiting for her and, when she approached, quietly led her into an office at the end of the hall. She entered the equally quiet, equally cold room and sat in an empty seat on the other side of a large white steel and wood desk. When Clara looked back at the dog, she found it had disappeared.

She settled her bag onto her lap, feeling a modicum of safety return, as though the bag were a shield. Her eyes fell on the giant picture of her that was projected onto the wall.

Someone was here. Someone had to have opened up her files. Her fingers threaded together as her unease gradually returned. She was completely out of her element and hated looking at the giant image of herself.

The girl on the wall was who she used to be before she'd sworn off men, before she vowed several unbreakable oaths. She was smiling, happy. That girl had been engaged; she still had a bright future. Had the prospect of a normal life.

Clara clenched her fingers together tighter.

And waited.

Chapter Three

• • • •

Reid straightened his lab coat and flexed his muscles, loosening them. He entered his office, startling the girl who pretended to be unafraid. Clara Anne Warren.

"Clara?" he asked with a modicum of boredom. She stood and he waved her back into her seat as he walked around his desk and sat down. Her hands were clenched, holding a purse that had seen better days.

"Yes."

She visibly swallowed and Reid opened up his wristcon to take notes. He didn't need to, but it always unnerved hopefuls when things were being written about them that they couldn't see. Half the time he was filling out material requisition forms for the facility. The other half of the time it was Sudoku.

"Why are you here?" he asked without pleasantries.

He glanced up as Clara fumbled to find the right words. Her tongue slipped across her bottom lip. "For the same reason anyone would come here."

Right. "You'd be surprised, Ms. Warren. Men and women have a lot of different reasons why they come here."

"They do?"

"Yes. Shelter, protection, to have a child, to fuck a Cyborg," Reid mused with a shrug, watching a blush spread across her cheeks. Why be subtle when the truth was there for all to hear?

"Oh... well, I want to have a child."

"Good to know. We're not a charity." He brought up her file to double-check her answers. "Why?"

19

"Why?" she asked with a hint of confusion.

"Yes. Why do you want to have a child? Why do you want to have a cybernetic child? What brought you here?"

"I've always wanted to have a family. I never had one growing up and I love children. I've tried... before this," she looked around the room briefly, "but it never worked out, it always failed. It's hard to explain."

"Nothing is hard to explain. You're choosing not to. If you can't answer my questions fully and without reservation then there's no reason to continue this conversation."

Her blush deepened. "I have a history of choosing the wrong men and one of them hurt me pretty bad." She swiped her fingers across her stomach. "I've tried over and over again. I guess I just really want a family. My own family. And right now I can't, so that's why I'm here."

Reid steepled his fingers and stared at Clara, who twitched with nerves despite trying not to. She smelled good, she responded well, and although she was nervous he could hear the truth in her voice. Already, his need to delve deeper and provide protection slithered through him.

He needed to get Clara the hell out of his facility.

"You were stabbed," he stated rather than questioned.

She blanched but recovered quickly.

"Yes."

"In the abdomen?"

Clara nodded. "And below it..."

"It appears that's the reason why you can't get pregnant."

"It would seem so," she snapped.

"So, the real reason you're here is to get reconstructive surgery." His voice hardened.

"Yes and no. I do need reconstructive surgery and I can't afford it, but I'm here to have a child, regardless of whether it's human, Cyborg, or half-breed."

"But you do *need* reconstructive surgery, right?"

Clara shuffled in her seat. "Yes. I do need the surgery, but the ability to have a child is the most important thing to me."

Reid lowered his tablet and looked her directly in the eye. "Even if that child is cybernetic? You know what that means, don't you? It means that your child would have cells unlike any other human. They won't be wholly human, but half machine. And even though they won't have *metal* within their bodies, their cells would have technology fused within, making them nano-capable. Those nanoparticles belong to the government, which means..."

"I'd have to share parenting rights with the government," she finished for him.

"Yes. If you were to get pregnant during your stay here, your child would be monitored for the rest of its life. Their free will they would retain, but they would always be accompanied by cybernetic scientists. You would be their mother, you would be their family, you would be free to offer your opinion on every decision, but that's all you would have. Do you understand? Your rights end there."

Reid was being harsh. This was the point where every woman cowed and decided that they needed to think whether or not this program was for them. This is where the conversation always ended.

Clara pursed her lips and glanced up at her image on the wall beside him. Her pupils clouded and her face wavered, and her fingers twitched before she locked eyes with him again.

He was reminded of the way she had reacted to his beast. How, even though she was afraid and uncertain, she held her ground.

"I understand. When can we start?" Her countenance hardened.

I really need to get her out of here.

"That's good to know," his voice strained. "Your file says you don't have a partner but you were recently engaged. What happened?"

"He broke it off."

"Why?"

"He was an idiot."

"... So you're single?"

"Yes."

"Good."

"Why is that good?" Clara ran her fingers through her hair and repositioned her sunglasses over her head. He tracked every single movement she made whether he liked it or not.

"Couples have a problem, typically, with the fact that another man's sperm would be within their wife... or partner. It's caused issues in the past and so we only take single women now." Were it his partner, he'd have that same problem too.

"Doesn't seem like you take anyone now," she murmured.

Reid smiled. "Is that sarcasm?"

"No, no it's not. It's just very quiet here. What's your name again?"

He lazily pointed to the tag at the corner of his desk.

"Dr. Reid Canis?"

"Supposedly."

The look on her face as she stared at his tag was unreadable. Suddenly, Clara wasn't really looking at his tag anymore and he found himself intrigued. Her gaze went far away, Reid noted, and far from him. Her pulse quickened to a beat in his eardrums. *What's wrong with my goddamn name?*

"What is the likelihood of having a child here?" she asked.

His lips twitched. "Not high—not yet—but we're always trying new things and improving our process. Artificial wombs—the ones used to create Cyborgs—are unbelievably expensive and as a result, Cyborgs are rarely created anymore. However, there is still a strong need for their services. Even with an artificial womb—which is what the process we use requires—the likelihood that the DNA involved has a one and twenty percent chance of success. The cells usually die."

Clara finally looked up from his tag to turn her gaze back to him. The lumpy hobo bag in her lap spilled over to one side. He wanted to know what was in it.

"Natural wombs," she balled her hands into her shirt, "wouldn't up the chance if it's the cells that are failing?"

"True," he said. "Unless we use the mother's DNA to create the Cyborg."

"I don't understand. I thought that Cyborgs were only created with perfected DNA. I don't think the average woman has perfect DNA. *I* don't have perfect DNA."

"And why we don't take human candidates, usually." He smiled and she sat back as her focus lowered to his mouth. "So you know something about us."

Reid enjoyed watching his words sink in.

For one moment, Clara Anne Warren had achieved a sense of calm, but as the realization of what he said struck her, her mouth parted and her heart rate skyrocketed. That tiny reprieve of calmness evaporated.

"You're a Cyborg?"

Reid pressed his thumb over his lips. "Yes."

She took him in, checked him over while he did the same.

"It's not obvious, is it?"

She didn't answer him.

Her hair tumbled from behind her sunglasses to dance around her shoulders, blonde like a fading sun. The tart smell of berries reached his nose. Shell-shocked was the only way to describe her expression.

"I suppose it wouldn't be. Part of the idea is being able to blend in," he continued. "For my model, at least."

Clara licked her lips and he wondered if they would taste like the tart fruit she smelled of. Reid stiffened. *Where did that thought come from?* He wasn't surprised by her reaction. Cyborgs were fucking rare, practically myths to some people, and legends to others. The likelihood of encountering one was minuscule; the likelihood of encountering one near or on Earth was even smaller.

"Am I supposed to have sex with *you*?"

Reid choked.

* * * *

HER BAG SPILLED ONTO the floor. The man across from her opened and closed his mouth like a guppy and the intimidation she felt before was replaced with horrified embarrassment.

"No," he cleared his throat. "You won't be touched... by me, or anyone else."

Clara leaned over and picked her purse up off the floor. Her eyes remained on the man—Cyborg—who suddenly couldn't stop moving. "So, I'm part of the program?"

"No—"

"But you said no one would touch me." Her resolve hardened.

He scowled at her but she held her ground. Clara didn't know the rules for candidacy for the program and she knew she was definitely not the ideal candidate by a long shot. That didn't matter to her.

She shuddered to think what would happen if she left the facility without a contract.

Dr. Canis clasped his hands and put his elbows on the desk, leaning toward her. "It's not that easy."

"But... you said—"

"I know what I said." His face went dark, and she her breath caught in her throat. "There is a lot to consider when joining this program. Both from my perspective as an administrator and yours as a potential candidate." Reid seemed to grow more imposing as he talked. *How did I ever see him as just a man?* "If you sign the contract, it's for three months. Three tries. You'll be monitored constantly. You'll have no privacy."

"Why?"

"We would have to make sure that you did nothing to harm yourself or jeopardize the process." He made a show of flicking through some digital paperwork that she couldn't see. It made her angry how cavalier he was being. She knew all this going in and she understood the lack of privacy, but she didn't like it.

"Who would be watching me?"

He looked up and pinned her with his black eyes. She barely held back a shiver and it wasn't from the frigid atmosphere of the room. Would he be watching her?

"A.I. mainly. Your doctor will have access but only under certain protocols would he observe. But if you do something that has negative effects on the process, the A.I. and I will be notified. But, you should know that there will be daily check-ups and your health would be completely in our hands."

"What does that mean?" *You better not be serious, asshole.*

"You won't be able to leave once you've signed, at least not the grounds. Your diet and your daily activities will be monitored as well as your vitamin intake, chemicals, and mental stability. Any personal freedoms will be surrendered for the duration of your contract."

It's worth it. She told herself. *If I'm able to get the surgery and gain the ability to have children for three months of captivity... it's more than worth it.* Hell, she'd resigned herself to a lot longer if it meant that she would get what she wanted. It wasn't like she hadn't been a captive before. At least this time she stood to benefit from it.

"What happens when the three months are up?"

"That depends. If you're pregnant, you'll have to remain here for the entire cycle and the months following."

Clara looked away and to her image projected onto the wall.

She had been happy then, at that moment, with her fiancé. He was a good man—unlike Santino—a decent one and she would've been happy with him, happy living a quiet, normal life even if she would never be able to have children. At least she would've had somebody to care for. Someone to care for her.

Could she do it?

I could be beholden, my child could be beholden to the government for years to come.

If she were able to get pregnant here, her child would be strong, be healthy, have access to a great education, and would never have to deal with the slums and the wasteland that remained of Middle America.

She could do it. Her child would have the world at its fingertips and technology in its body that would outlive this age and the next.

She looked back at the man across from her. *I could deal with this asshole too.* If it meant reaching her goal, she could. But she couldn't deny the hollow feeling in her gut and the intimidation she felt under his gaze.

He really is a Cyborg...

"Where do I sign?"

The Cyborg rose from his seat with a scowl.

Chapter Four

· · · ·

"Twenty-four hours." *Twenty-four damning hours.* Reid powered down his office technology and rounded his desk, resting his hand on the back of Clara's chair in an effort to lead her out of the room. His fingers brushed her silken blond hair.

She looked up at him, her body stiff under his shadow. "For what?"

"Until you're allowed to sign."

She scrambled out of her seat to follow him as he left the room. His hackles raised, annoyed, frustrated, and his nostrils filled with the smell of fruit. Her footsteps sounded behind him.

"I'm ready now."

"Standard procedure."

"I don't need it. I've thought this through. I'm a hundred percent certain I want to join the program."

His teeth ground together. Reid had made a mistake, because her question shook him. *'I have to have sex with you?'*

No, Clara, but now that you mention it... He wanted to shake her words out of his head and dig his claws into the cement outside. Reid clenched his hands, making sure his nails remained retracted. It had been decades since he had last been with a woman.

"It doesn't matter. Protocol," he gritted out as they entered the reception area. He walked past the desk and moved toward the door. "Go back to your hotel or hostel and think about it.

Come back this time tomorrow if you're certain." He opened the door for her. A wave of arid, stifling, hellish heat blasted him and with it came the desert powder. Reid turned to face her. "Good day, Ms. Warren."

"I don't..."

She stopped just out of his reach and eyed the exit with wariness. He couldn't read her.

"You don't *what*?"

"I don't have a place to go."

Reid pulled his gaze from hers and looked at her vehicle on the far side of the parking lot.

"There's a place not five miles past the gates. Take a left, you can't miss it."

"I don't have any money."

Don't. Don't play the hero. Her words set off a war inside of him.

"Please let me sign today..."

He let go of the door and dropped his arms. The outside vanished at his back.

"Do you need money, Clara?"

She took a slight step away from him and he couldn't blame her. Reid had his walls up for a reason. But there was something about the way she smelled—fresh and alluring—and when she turned her big violet eyes toward his, he found himself drowning in their depths. He wanted to close the short distance between them and nuzzle up against her.

"I... err, what?"

Reid flicked on his wristcon and brought up his personal finances—not the facility's, but his. "How much?"

"I'm not taking money from you."

"You need the time to think." *I have plenty to spare.* He kept his eyes off of hers.

"I don't. I really don't. If you need to give me time, give me twenty minutes, an hour, I'll stay here in reception and think about it. I'll make a pro-con chart."

"Would you still say that if I told you that you *did* have to have sex with a Cyborg?"

He told himself it was to send her away, to scare her off, and that it wasn't because he yearned to know the answer.

She scrunched her features and checked him out. "Would it have to be *you*?"

"Does it matter?"

"Yes."

Reid sighed and walked toward the desk, bringing up the screen without questioning further. It was better that he didn't know the answer.

"Sign here." He stepped aside and indicated the projected document.

He watched as Clara visibly shook herself and approached it. She read over the clauses and signed the file, her lithe finger dancing across the air. His jaw ticked. *Sign both of our time away, Clara dear.* The next three months might be hard for her, but it would be hell for him.

Reid was already growing accustomed to her presence. The sound of her steps. The sway of her curves hidden behind loose clothing. Before long, if he wasn't careful, he wouldn't want to let her out of his sight.

He powered down the document. "Do you have a personal IP address?"

"Yeah." She pulled out her network card and handed it to him. He noticed that she didn't pull out a personal wristcon or tablet. It was almost unheard of to not have a device on hand.

Reid took her card, careful not to touch her fingers, and memorized it instantly. Her version of the contract was sent immediately to *her*... wherever or whatever device that carried her data.

"Everything's been sent to you. Follow me." He moved back toward the exit.

"You could be less demanding. A *please* can go a long way."

Once again he held the door for her. "No."

"It would make you less of a jerk." She stepped past him. "Where are we going?"

"To get your things. I'm not a jerk."

"Hah!"

"I'm a realist. It's not my problem you don't like hearing the truth."

Clara shot him a killing glare at his back, one he couldn't see, but could feel.

Her vehicle was an age old, maybe even older than him. As he neared, he seeded into its mechanics and found parts that had, indeed, been around longer than he had. It was like the technology of Earth, where waste was no longer waste but only a set of materials that could be utilized in another fashion. Everything was recycled.

Still, the outside rust of the vehicle made him feel grimy. No Cyborg liked being near old technology for long; it was the encroaching decay that every machine would one day go through. That one day he'd go through. It was too much like climbing into a cadaver.

Reid knew it was still operating, or else she wouldn't be here, but he also knew it probably shouldn't be.

He grabbed her bags with a small protest from her and led Clara back into the facility, through reception, and in the direction opposite his office. They passed several locked doors where he had her scan her fingerprints for future access and entered the currently unused residency section of the building.

"This is your room." He unlocked her door and held it open. She walked by him again and her nearness made him stiffen.

Reid followed her in, leaving the door open behind him, and placed her bags on the bed. Clara did a three-sixty and looked at the space. He tried seeing it through her eyes.

There was one large white bed, an alcove with a food replicator and some adjoining appliances, one round corner table with three chairs, empty wall panels, an open door to the bathroom, and one large mounted television wall screen. Everything was in shades of cold and colder greys. It was industrial, clean, and as far from comfortable as possible.

She faced him with another unreadable expression. He wanted to know what was in her head.

"What now?" she asked.

"Settle in, get a good night's rest. Tomorrow you'll have reconstructive surgery. Don't eat anything tonight."

Her eyes widened and she glanced down at her belly.

His need to pry amplified with each passing second. *I have to leave.* He didn't want to leave. The part of him that was a shepherd wanted to stay and guard, protect, and bond. His fists clenched at his sides despite his need to close the distance and continue to sniff her.

"So soon?"

"Yes. Do you have any questions before I go? I assume you know how to work the amenities in here?" *I need to get out of here. I need to leave. Now.* It wasn't his place.

She briefly looked around the room again. "Can I leave the room?"

"You can go anywhere you want that allows you access. If you have it, the doors will open as you near," he said, with strained patience. "Some rooms are locked, other living spaces, the laboratories, my office... but you can go outside as far as the first security checkpoint. If you choose to go beyond that point, an alarm will sound, and your contract will be forfeit and you'll be fined for your time here."

Clara licked her lips and he watched, wanting to lick them himself. *What's wrong with me?*

The need to bond with another being had never been so demanding before. She was dangerous because of it, dangerous to him. Berries continued to spin through his systems; images of strawberries, raspberries, and blackberries were in his head.

"All right..."

Reid turned to leave but before he closed the door behind him, she stopped him again.

"Wait! Where is everyone else?"

"There isn't anyone else."

"Why? What happened? I thought there would be so many... I expected a wait list, selection... I thought this entire process was going to be so different than what it has been."

"Nothing happened." His hand tightened on the door handle. "We don't get many applicants here. We don't need them.

CBF stopped advertising years ago and the main facility is now on Gliese."

"So... I'm alone?" her question came out warily. He couldn't blame her. He would be concerned if he were alone as well... alone and with a strange man, a Cyborg she disliked, no less.

"We get temporaries here occasionally." He felt the need to reassure her. "Applicants from Gliese that are transferred here for further testing. It's the nature of the beast—of science—the equipment installed here, well, can't be moved without an extreme amount of effort. This facility has become more of a laboratory than anything since the war. Can you imagine trying to transfer the hadron collider into space? Some machines—labs—aren't meant to move."

"Oh..."

"Goodnight, Clara." Reid closed the door and made his escape, filtering out everything about her from his systems: her smell, her mannerisms, even the few interactions they had that had softened him, and buried it all under a mountain of code.

By the time he reached the parking lot he had stripped out of his suit and was surging forward into the vast grounds and setting sun.

What better way to tire out a dog but with a long run in the fading desert heat?

Chapter Five

• • • •

The next morning, Clara opened her bedroom door to find the mechanical dog sitting in the hallway. Its eyes were black, intelligent, and oddly comforting.

"Hi?" she greeted it and cocked her head, leaning out to look down both ends of the hallway. "Did you chime the door?"

She stepped aside and allowed the animal to enter her space. The clicks of its metal paws and curved, pointed nails tapped on the cement floor and into her room.

"If you're to lead me to medical, I'm almost ready." She watched the dog sit down beyond her door. "You must be one of the androids that Dr. Canis mentioned," she murmured more to herself.

Although she'd found no cameras the night before, she knew she was being watched. Based on the conversation she had with the Cyborg yesterday, there was some A.I. technology *somewhere* keeping tabs on her. The lack of privacy was vaguely unsettling but it didn't bother her as much as she expected.

Maybe because she chose it. *Whatever gets me closer to my dreams.*

Clara eyed the dog. It followed her with its eyes as she walked a semi-circle around it.

It was large—larger than any dog she had ever seen before—but then again, it was a mechanical one. The sky was the limit when it came to fabricating new creatures.

It acted like a dog, it looked like a dog, but it seemed far more than what it appeared. *Never underestimate an android: you never know what they're programmed for.*

Still, she liked having the companion with her; it made it less lonely and it made her feel safe. She took a step toward the canine and reached her hand out. It nuzzled her fingers and Clara smiled, moving her hand over its head and down its back.

Her phone rang, breaking the moment.

The dog shifted its gaze toward her purse where her phone buzzed. Its mouth opened to reveal sharp, metallic teeth.

Clara swallowed, left her new scary friend, and sourced out her phone. *Pecos PD.* She answered it.

"Hello, this is Clara."

"Clara, it's Marsha, we spoke yesterday. Can you verify your information please?" The woman had a strange sense of urgency to her voice. She sat down on the edge of her bed knowing she wasn't going to like what she was about to hear. Clara stated her information.

"What's wrong?" She couldn't keep the breathy anxiety out of her question.

"We lost track of Santino."

"Already? How? You said only yesterday you were tracking him in Spring Grove." Her foot tapped the floor as of rush of fear pulsed through her. She tried to shake it, but it didn't go way.

"Yes, he was there until his personal IP network information went offline."

"Couldn't that mean... that he could be dead?" *Please let him be dead.*

"Yes, but even so there are still traces... We're worried about your safety. We'd like you to come down to the station."

No one's worried about my safety.

Clara had to remind herself that Marsha was only trying to do her job. But something felt off. The years hadn't gone by without her learning a thing or two to protect yourself. She took a moment before she answered, calculating her response.

"Okay," she agreed. Her mouth ran dry but she still swallowed despite her parched throat.

"We'll be able to keep you safe here and set up a protective patrol. I'll come and get you. Where are you?"

Clara licked her lips. "I'm out, but I'll head there right away. Are you sure Santino couldn't be dead?" Clara's stared at the dog which stood right beside her. It had moved closer without her realizing it. *How did I not notice?*

Marsha spoke up, "We can't take chances with your safety, Clara. Are you sure you don't need an escort? Just tell me where you are."

Nowhere I'm telling you. "On the road. I'll be there soon." Clara hung up and squeezed the small, archaic phone in her hand. An inexpensive model, a throwback to a more primitive era of technological evolution. Vintage was cheap and always in style.

Santino knows. Marsha and the Pecos PD could no longer help her. *It's only a matter of time before he finds me.* A black light flashed, catching her eyes and driving them back to the giant metal canine beside her.

I'm safe here, she told herself as she stared at the beast. *For the next three months, he can't get to me.* For the next three months, she'd have a frightening giant metal dog to protect her. It did come with a warning sign.

Clara dropped her phone on the bed and walked into the bathroom, intent on washing away her fear, worry, and the ill-timed conversation with Marsha.

She wouldn't let it affect her chances.

• • • •

THE DOG WAS GONE WHEN she left the bathroom but the moment she stepped back into her room, another chime sounded for access.

This is it. I'm about to be fixed.

Clara ran her fingers through her blow-dried hair, feeling alone now that her companion had once again vanished, and opened the door.

To *him*. Her heart skipped a beat.

A very angry, very cocky looking Cyborg doctor stood on the other side.

Previous worries drained away as Dr. Canis, once again, took up all the space and all her thoughts. He fit the door frame, shoulder to panel, his pushed back hair touched the top.

His eyes narrowed on hers and she narrowed hers right back. He eventually looked away and swept his gaze across her room.

She had neither unpacked nor made a mess. She preferred order and cleanliness since everything else around her seemed to be a chaos that she couldn't control.

And that chaos extended to the extremely attractive man in front of her. His appearance alone was enough to intimidate her. *I shouldn't be allowed in his presence...*

"Is it time?" she asked, breaking the silence.

"Yes, follow me." His voice was clipped and strained and she didn't know why. In fact, she didn't know why he was here at all. Clara thought, hoped, that she would no longer be dealing with him.

"You're taking me? I thought there'd be another human... an android at least?"

"No. Only me. Who would want a human doctor anyways? That would be like asking a toddler to finger-paint your house and the androids are dealing with more important things."

Wooow. Clara rolled her eyes.

Only him? It dawned on her. *Only him. Only him...* A shiver ran through her. *Where's the dog when I need protection?*

She looked at the man walking in front of her, the meticulously arranged dark suit he wore and the obvious musculature that was barely restrained beneath it. Her stomach grew queasy with butterflies as she openly gawked, not even hiding it. The only thing that stopped her from running back to her room was the cold indifference that wafted from him in frigid waves; she was thankful for it because if he were a charmer, she might've been lured in.

Somehow, her skin warmed up despite the rapidly chilling temperature that only fell lower as they walked further into the building.

They stopped at a door. *Only him?* The flutter in her belly vanished as reality sank in.

She was in a daze as he typed in a code and a laser flashed over his face. The door opened shortly after. The medical lab revealed itself in all its pomp and sterile circumstantial glory.

He was her doctor. The handsome asshole was her fucking doctor.

Reid led her from the hallway and into a small private space, no different than a number of surgical labs she'd been in before except for the streamlined technology that assembled into one jumble: an expensive room with an extensive history of pain. But all she could really focus on was the cushy cryopod that took up a third of the room.

The pod she was soon to be lying on with him hovering over her.

Reality was such a nasty bitch.

Somehow, Clara knew that this moment was going to stay with her for a very, very long time. Even if it weren't a pivotal point where she took control of her life, it would remain erect as a precariously *wrong* situation. She glanced between the dangerously attractive man and the prominent oval medical bed.

Her mind wandered to all the wrong places. *I've always had problems wanting the wrong men.*

She already knew the answer to her question but she asked it anyway, "You're my doctor?"

He didn't turn to face her. Instead, he pulled off his jacket in such a mechanically indifferent way that she wanted to watch him shed all of his clothes off just to see if his control and authority went to all aspects of his life.

She pressed her legs together and hated herself for it.

"Yes, Ms. Warren, I am. Does that bother you?"

The door behind her shut, startling her. Once again she wished for the dog.

It does bother me, asshole. But it didn't stop her from watching him step into a glass enclosure in the corner that sterilized his hands and clothing. Their eyes met through the glass.

"No. It doesn't bother me." She pulled her gaze away from his and rejoiced in her small victory. Her hands clenched at her sides and sweat coated her palms. *I can do this. I'm safe here. I'm safe with him. A Cyborg doctor would never botch this. He's done this before.*

Don't freak out.

Exhilaration slithered through her.

It's really happening.

Her lips lifted. Her hands slid over her belly and its soft rounded curve to rub the spot where her scars were. Her wariness vanished, and suddenly she wanted to jump up and down and scream to the skies and move on with her life.

"Are you okay?"

Yes! "Yes, I'm more than okay." She didn't try to suppress her smile and was taken aback when the Cyborg flashed her one in return.

"I guess my excitement is catching," she laughed. He turned away and slipped on a pair of gloves.

"It is, and if you're ready we can get this over with."

Clara nodded and wanted to dance. *Afterward*, she told herself. *Once I'm healed, I'll dance the night away where no one can see me.*

Next, Dr. Canis helped her into the same sterilization chamber, his eyes locked on hers as a gaseous mist coated her skin and clothes. When it cleared and the chamber reopened, he gave her a plastic-sealed medical shift to put on. He then donned a crisp white lab coat.

She moved to the corner, turned her back, and began to peel out of her clothes.

A cough sounded behind her. "I can leave."

Clara didn't care; her giddiness and the nearness of her goals were at the forefront of her thoughts, not the handsome man who was locked with her in the medical lab.

She shook her head without looking back. "No point, I don't want to waste time, just turn your back if it's modesty you're worried about, it's not like you won't see me in a short while anyway."

She didn't wait for a response, instead, pulling off her clothes and folding them. She slid on the shift and smoothed the wrinkles down.

Her skin was covered in gooseflesh and her nipples were taut, poking through the cloth of the medical dress. It was from the cold, and once again she told herself she didn't care. *I'm going to be fixed!*

Who cared that it was going to be a dangerously handsome, asshole Cyborg doctor—created to wage war—that was going to fix her? She squeezed her thighs together and told herself it was because of her lack of dress, and not because there was barely a scrap of tissue paper cloth between the two of them.

When he turned around and looked at her, she was ready for his cold indifference, not for the warmth and comfort that shone in his eyes. Eyes he kept fixed on her face.

Why does that disappoint me? Her grin didn't budge as she scrambled to the bed. He offered his hand to help her into it. She clasped it without a thought.

The moment they touched, something shifted, something unassuming and potent as his large hand tightened around her small one. It wasn't the gentle stiffening of a helpful hand, but the tightening of a hand that wanted to feel more.

They locked eyes and a rush of heat slithered through her. So many shivers for so many different reasons, but as she stared into the depths of his dark eyes, a sense of familiarity poked her memories.

Before she could place it—and the look he gave her—he helped her maneuver into the oval pod. When she was lying down—at her most vulnerable with her heart racing and ready to burst from her chest—a twinge of nervousness returned.

He still has my hand...

"Don't be nervous. You're safe with me." His face softened and a lock of hair fell over his face. Clara nodded and swallowed, and held back from reaching up and brushing his rebel hair away from his brow.

"I feel safe," she mustered out. It was the truth. He gave her hand a slight squeeze. So handsome, so wrong. *So wrongly handsome.* She missed the asshole because she had no defenses against the kindness.

"This won't take long," he told her. "You'll feel some discomfort when you wake up and you won't be able to lift anything heavy for a day or so, but I promise there won't be any pain."

"I like that promise." Clara couldn't take her eyes off his face and she didn't want him to let her go. "Will you be here when I wake up?"

"Yes, I'll be here."

She briefly closed her eyes with relief. "Thank you, Dr. Canis."

"Call me, Reid."

"Reid," she said softly.

Her body heated outward from where they were connected and she craved more of it. But Reid released her with a soft caress over her knuckles and Clara realized as he moved away that what she felt was the need to be held, comforted. Well, by the fantasy of him in her head. She was freezing and for a brief moment, he had warmed her up.

Reid had also given her a lifeline of hope that not all men out there were bad and...that was dangerous.

He's dangerous.

She shook her head and looked at the room around her. *This is neither the place nor the time to be thinking about men.*

He turned back to her with a scanner in his hand and ran it over her body; the medical feed appeared on a screen beyond her view. His hand held her gaze, clasped over the device he moved up and down her body, and her toes curled, thinking, imagining, that he was doing it for an entirely different reason.

A non-medical reason.

What the fuck is wrong with me? She closed her eyes.

Reid was being entirely professional and she was on the verge of being an aggressor. Clara wanted to open up her legs and ask for a quick, blissful, non-committal climax to get whatever she was feeling out of her system.

Her eyes snapped open and back to him. His focus was on the readings, not her. His attention wasn't on her.

Clara smiled, knowing he wasn't looking, and imagined the scenario and shifted her hips a little without meaning to.

I'm fairly certain he'd kick me out of the facility if I did that. She bit back a laugh but couldn't stop the yawning ache between her legs and the idea of her fantasy coming to life.

"Are you ready?" His voice was rough and deeper than before. Her pulse skipped as she was thrown from her thoughts.

The softness of his features had vanished and his eyes had grown dark and menacing; his muscles twitched and strained under the lab coat. He looked mad, yet restrained, and Clara resisted the urge to cover herself up behind her arms.

There's no way he knows what I was thinking.

"I'm ready," she whispered, letting her previous thoughts burn up in flames.

He brushed his finger over the back of her hand, dousing that fire. Before the pod closed up behind a glass shield and a euphoric mist filled up the space, he did it once more. Clara snatched her hand away from the contact. Their eyes met. *He touched me by choice? Again?*

She didn't get a chance to ask why before the glass cut her off and another, thicker gas filled in around her. She sucked it into her lungs. It calmed her heart, took away her excitement, and her adrenaline; her body grew heavy while her thoughts went airy and light.

That touch of his fingers stayed with her until she succumbed to sleep.

• • • •

CLARA WENT UNDER IN less than a minute. Reid studied her vitals. And when the mists dissipated and her body came back into view, a surge of primal instinct coursed him. It felt like a bullet to his gut and he took a step back. *Her smell...*

Something he did, she liked; he had made a mistake. He clenched his gloved hands around the scanner, hearing a plastic crack. Even now he could smell her excitement, the heady scent of arousal. His body hardened, his cock stiffened, and he swore to himself that it would pass as quickly as it had begun.

He turned around and counted to ten. Slowly. Then he did it again. It was enough for him to regain control over his beast.

His fingers relaxed at his sides and he sighed in relief as her smell was replaced by the clinical and antiseptic gas released from the machine. He looked upon her with indifference. At least that's what he tried to convince himself of.

The glass lifted away and he loosened the straps on either side of her shift, revealing the lower half of her body.

Reid stopped. He stared. The metal plates in his body expanded.

Every shred of control he had gained back vanished as his eyes traced her pelvic area. An anger rose inside him and his coding flared red alert throughout his mainframe. Clara's belly was covered in crisscrossing white scars, a web of uncontrolled frenzy. It was chaotic, and even though they were healed, he could feel the pain of her old wounds inside him. The scars ran from one hipbone to the other and down below her pelvis where they vanished beneath the band of her underwear.

He'd read that she'd been stabbed—it was in her file—and even then it had angered him, but seeing them was worse.

A need arose in him to protect what was now under his care and his authority.

Reid wanted to shift his face and growl, to feel the rumbles of his anger vibrate through his body. He wanted to shift and seek out her attacker, whoever he was, and stalk him in the dead of night. He wanted to rip out the man's throat and feel the slick essence of that bastard's life force bleed over his gums.

He could already taste the coppery tang of the man's blood in his mouth.

But it wasn't his place to insert himself into Clara's life or her past. It certainly wasn't his place to seek out her enemies. Reid allowed his heart to freeze over again. Right now, there were better things to do with his time: to do for her.

I can heal her, and I can make her future more secure, but I can't save her.

He hooked one finger in her underwear and pulled the top down to see how far down her scars went.

His mouth watered as a delicious, tart scent flooded his nose, and he ran his gloved fingertip through the soft, groomed curls between her legs. The scarring vanished within and left only small trails of white where her hair no longer grew.

So soft. He traced the scars with his finger until it stopped an inch above her clit. His gaze locked on it, pink and perfect, and unhidden. He leaned forward, wondering what it tasted like, what *she* tasted like and if it was anything like her scent. *She's just waiting to be played with.*

Her pretty pink clit looked like a perfect target for his mouth. He wanted to practice.

Reid jerked back as if he'd been burned. The seam of her panties righted back into its position over her, hiding her from his prying eyes. *What the fuck is wrong with me?*

His jaw ticked as he stretched his tense muscles and he composed himself.

He got to work.

Chapter Six

• • • •

Reid was sitting at her side, waiting for her to awaken when his wristcon buzzed. He glanced down at the screen, noting that the one human guard in his employment had sent him a message, and opened communication.

'There's a woman out here insisting that she see Clara.'

He messaged back. *'Who is she?'* A moment later her IP address flooded through and he had all the information he needed.

Marsha Tannett of Pecos PD. He knew of her, having listened in on Clara's phone call that morning. Her file checked out; Marsha was a sworn officer of the law. Why would someone from old Texas be out in no man's desert America? Furthermore, how did the cop know Clara was here? *Clara hadn't disclosed her location.*

The image of her scars rose up in his mind. His gaze shifted back to the sleeping beauty breathing softly in the pod next to him. An innocent who had been hurt by the worst of human society, the dregs.

Reid left her side and headed for the gate, annoyed.

"Let her through the first barrier but tell her to wait. I'll be right there." He was out of the facility, through the parking lot, and past all the inner gates and checkpoints within moments. He smelled Marsha the cop long before he saw her.

Anxiety and fear. He should've known.

Somehow, in one day, he had become embroiled with women who needed his help. Reid sighed. He needed to make this quick so he could get back to Clara's side before she woke.

A woman in her late thirties stood outside the vehicle. He looked beyond at the border guard and gave him a nod before he addressed the woman.

"Marsha?" He stepped right outside her personal bubble and she took a step back. No protector of the law let a stranger get close. But he had the upper hand, always had and always would.

Cyborgs outranked cops, preprogrammed with the laws that governed Earth and its people, and although he abided by its laws, there were others that took precedence.

The woman's hand drifted over the gun belt at her hip. "Yes." Her voice was strained and her lips were dry. "Who are you?"

"I'm in charge of this facility and I've been told you're here for one of my patients?" He canted his head.

She nodded and peered around them, casting a quick glance back toward the security gate. It was only for a second, but he'd noticed, and before she could meet his eyes again, he turned around and looked where she had.

The dust rolled off in waves far out into the arid wastes beyond and factories and ramshackle buildings dotted the landscape throughout. Reid scanned the horizon.

She's being watched, tracked... He knew it. The whistle of the desert wind blew across his ears, bringing with it the creeping knowledge that they weren't alone.

There wasn't another lifeform nearby and it wasn't the security guard or Clara. And although Marsha didn't have a gun to her head didn't mean she wasn't in trouble. Reid hoped that whatever was watching them knew that he knew. They were on his radar.

She cleared her throat. "What are you looking at?"

"The same thing you were."

"There's nothing out there—"

"Then why are you here?" he cut her off, turning her way, startling her.

"Sir, I work with the Pecos Police Department and I've been in contact with Clara for quite some time—"

"Why?"

She licked her lips and shifted her stance, her legs widening, readying for a standoff. "That's not for me to say. Who are you again? I don't believe I got your name."

"Does it matter? You're on my ground and you're a fucking liar. You know what I am right?"

She visibly checked him out and her hands clenched at either side of her waist; the knuckles over her gun were white. "I don't care what you are. My job doesn't concern you. My job concerns the safety of the citizens in my jurisdiction."

"But we're not in your jurisdiction and I'm only going to ask you one more time. Why are you here?" Reid said slowly, deliberately.

"Sir—"

In a flash, he grabbed hold of the cop, locked her arms behind her back, and disarmed her of her weapons. Reid let her go. She scrambled back with a gasp and moved to defend herself, but it was too late.

Her gun and the bullets hit the ground at their feet as she spun to get inside her car. He slapped his hand against her door and stopped it from opening, leaving an indent in the middle.

"If this is how you want to play it, we'll play it."

"I don't think you understand that you just threatened a cop," she said in a rush, and he could smell the fear waft between them.

She took a deep breath and he commended her for keeping her cool. "Look," she said with a shaky breath. "I'm not here to cause problems, and Ms. Warren isn't answering her phone calls. If you allow me to speak to her, we can forget this exchange ever happened, and we'll both go our separate ways."

He towered over the woman and watched a single bead of sweat trickle from her hairline and over her forehead. She didn't smell sweet or delectable like Clara, but instead smelled of mint and cold steel, of thousands of hours burned out and wasted in a mediocre job. *Easy. The tired are always easy.*

Reid changed his demeanor, smiled, and nodded. It put her on edge. "Very well. I'll take you to her."

He walked toward the building, giving his back to whoever was watching them outside the gate. He heard the cop's footfalls behind him.

"Thank you... This won't take long."

"I wouldn't be so sure." He let Marsha through the second barricade without a background check. "Clara is recovering from surgery."

"She's *what*? Is she okay?"

"Yes, she's okay."

"She hasn't been hurt, has she?"

"Not unless you count everything she's already been through." He wondered how much Marsha knew about his breeder.

He glanced back at her. She tensed under his gaze and quickly looked back at the gate. Her movements twitched erratically, worsening with every step she furthered herself from it.

"Unless you count that..."

Reid held open the door to the reception. Marsha looked around with a shudder; her breath hitched. He made no move to enter and blocked the exit. When she got her fill of the quiet, cold place, she noticed she'd been trapped and turned back toward him. "This is a-a cybernetics facility."

"Yes."

Her mouth tightened into a straight line and a spark of judgment flashed over her eyes.

He continued, "Who's following you?"

Marsha startled but then stiffened. "I don't know you're talking about."

"You're in trouble. How is he threatening you?"

She licked her lips again and her hand dropped onto her belt where her weapon had been. "No one's threatening me. Take me to Clara."

"Is it your family?" Her jaw tightened. That was it; he had her. "Does he have them now?" He held her gaze. "Tell me," he demanded.

Marsha let out a long, shuddering sigh, deflated and suddenly haunted. "My girlfriend. He has my girlfriend."

Reid led her further into the room and asked her to sit. He sat across from her. Her face was nothing but grim although no tears showed in her eyes.

"What are the terms? Bring Clara out of here, to him? And you get your girlfriend back?"

She nodded.

Reid leaned back and rubbed his hand over his mouth in thought. His other hand tapped against the armrest. What had he got himself into?

"Do you have any idea where he could be keeping her?"

Her voice was tight, "No, but Santino recently got out of prison and checked into a halfway house in Dallas. Any resources he has would've had to be from someone he knew prior to his imprisonment or someone he met during."

Reid got up and walked behind the reception desk where he unlocked a drawer and pulled out a bottle of rum. He poured two lowball glasses before retaking his seat and handing one to her. She downed it in one go despite her teeth clanking into the cup. Reid held back a mirthless smile as he downed his own glass.

"Thanks," she said. He took her glass in response and set it aside.

"Santino?"

"I shouldn't have told you his name, I shouldn't be telling you any of this." Marsha ran her fingers across her temple. "My commander is going to be furious if he finds out but what am I to do? I'm in trouble regardless." She shook her head and cringed again. "I can't think straight. I want her back, and until she's back I can't think straight."

She hadn't answered his question but he let it slide. He was great at reading people, one of the best. He could do it without looking at them, without speaking to them, without hearing them, he could do it—read them just by scenting alone.

His senses were powerful, not only because of the tech inside of him but because of the DNA that was spliced into his cells. There was nothing quite like his sense of smell. His fingers twitched on his thigh. Even now he could smell her, Clara, from across the facility—behind a dozen doors, he could smell her.

Only a day had gone by and her scent made him uncomfortable. It did things to him he wasn't thrilled about.

She wants me.

He couldn't deny the slick arousal before her surgery and it had taken everything within himself to not shut her mouth with his, peel down her underwear, and slam himself inside of her. His lips twisted. How was he going to survive three months?

"Well, Marsha, I'm afraid I can't let you leave."

Being a dick came easy to him.

Chapter Seven

· · · ·

Clara woke slowly like the sun ascending the sky at dawn. She felt soft, comfortable, and the cloud she lay upon hugged and supported her in all the right places.

I'm on a cloud. She giggled to herself and blinked. She looked around and her eyes landed on Dr. Canis—no— Reid who sat beside her.

Her lips pressed up into a soft smile. "Are you on a cloud too?" She barely heard her own voice. His eyes flashed, black and dark. Not dawn, she mused to herself. Somehow, his eyes reminded her of something that she couldn't quite remember exactly, and despite the intense heat of his gaze, she couldn't look away.

"No, Clara, I'm not on a cloud." He leaned closer to her but she felt too good to move back.

"That's too bad, my cloud feels great." She laughed softly, feeling wonderful.

"Is that so?"

"I would never lie!" To prove it, she shook her hips, show-ing off the voluminous thing that covered every part of her. His eyes dipped down. She giggled and swayed them again. His Adam's apple bobbed over his throat and Clara had an urge to wrap her lips around it. "I wonder if it tastes like apples too?"

"What?" Reid's eyes shot back to hers.

"I said that out loud," she stated more for herself, then smiled. "Apples are food of the gods." Clara stretched as she said it, loving the feel of air on her skin.

"So are berries."

"Hmm. Yes. I agree."

His hand moved over her and pressed down on her torso right below her breasts to stop her from moving. It was like a burn, a brand, over the center of her body.

"Stop moving. You're still recovering. How do you feel?"

She reached up and gripped his wrist with both of her hands. His hand pressed further into her and it warmed her from the inside out.

"I feel good." Clara licked her lips and squeezed his wrist tighter. "You make me feel warm." He started to pull his hand away but she stopped him. "Don't go... I like it."

Reid relaxed by degrees. She could almost count each different expression he made as he went from heated strain to soft kindness. It moved her.

Clara closed her eyes hard and forced the pleasure-inducing haziness away. She let go of his wrist with remorse as hints of memory came back.

Surgery. I had surgery. Asshole doctor. Her hands dropped to her sides and she bit back her embarrassment. *Cyborg breeding facility...*

Fixed. Her eyes shot open, and she tried to lean up to look down at herself.

"Don't. There's time for that later." Reid stopped her this time with a hand on her shoulder.

She settled back down.

"Am I fixed?"

"Your surgery was successful. Fixed though? I don't know."

Asshole. But a sigh of relief escaped her and as she settled back into the cloud—medical bed, happy. She closed her eyes to bask by herself because this moment was hers and hers alone. *Reid won't ruin it. Won't let him.*

Yep. Those memories were really coming back now.

Clara suddenly felt his hands on her pelvis. Her eyes shot open to find Reid looking down at her belly. She was practically naked and this time awake for it. It made it difficult for her to stomach the situation, especially given that the procedure was over and an attractive, intimidating man stood over her. His fingers slipped across her skin, the sensation amazing under the haze of the painkillers.

Her scars!

"What are you looking at?" she asked quickly.

"Your incisions. They're healing well."

But my scars... Clara gulped. "That's good."

He met her eyes as he pulled down her shift and covered her back up. Everything he did was professional but somehow it felt extremely intimate and personal. If she could think properly, she knew her body would be flushed and her face would blush, and blushes never looked good on her. "When can I move again?"

"A day, maybe less."

"So soon?"

"You had a multimillion-dollar procedure done by two machines that cost half a billion. Yes, by this time tomorrow you could run a marathon."

Clara settled back, allowing her body to relax. "I like that. And having babies?"

His eyes hooded and she didn't know why. He danced between hot and cold one minute, a doctor the next, and a caring individual third.

"You could do that too tomorrow but I'd give it a couple more days," he leveled and turned away. She watched him peel off his latex gloves and throw them in the biohazard trash.

"I'd like to try as soon as possible."

He pulled off his lab coat, his movements restrained yet taut. "Tomorrow then," he said, voice cold.

She didn't let it bother her. Instead, leaned her head up to look down at her body and smiled. "Thank you."

"You're welcome."

Reid turned away from her, looking at something she couldn't see. Her eyes roved over his back, his butt and his wide stance. He looked like a soldier, a commander, a man who had an army at his beck and call.

She could imagine the beautiful outline of his muscles underneath his clothes, his tight skin, unmarked by human imperfection, powerful beyond belief. If she hadn't so recently sworn off men, she would've appreciated the commanding presence he exhibited, but now it served as merely a test of self-discipline and preservation.

Maybe he didn't count. *After all, Reid isn't technically a man. Why does he have to be so damn attractive?* she humphed to herself and looked up at the ceiling. The silence lingered and the pleasure faded. Every new moment that passed only made her more tired and irritable.

"Dr. Reid?"

"Yes?"

"How long have I been out... Under? I must've been asleep for the past decade."

"A little less than a day. The cybernetics can take a toll on one's body especially if you're not used to it. I kept you under to give you the extra rest."

"Oh." She processed his words and allowed them to sink again, but her mind was still on the edge of muddied and incoherent. If someone were to tell her dragons were real right now she would probably believe them. Fervently. Something was off... Her moods swung back and forth like a pendulum. "Where's all the blood?"

I'm so full of questions! She felt like a kid again.

Her vision swirled.

"The pod uses varying degrees of lasers when it comes to surgery. So do I. Your bedding remains clean."

His answer didn't answer much. Her eyes wavered back and forth across the stark room and she could've sworn she saw a dragon gliding lazily back and forth, taunting her like Reid's deep voice had.

"I don't like blood."

"Not many people do."

"Do you?" She gave up on the dragon.

"I'm indifferent to it."

Her vision steadied as she focused on him.

I used to be indifferent to it... She wouldn't let that thought continue. "I guess you'd have to not care about it if you're a doctor. A Cyborg as well."

"Some Cyborgs, Clara, love blood. I'm not one of them. I prefer cleanliness, good health, and order."

I prefer those things too, especially now that you said it. She jittered.

"I bet that you prefer those things in bed too," she laughed at her own joke, unfazed by her crassness and yet hoping that Reid responded to her in some way.

It was hard to form an opinion on someone who had such a wide range of temperament. Hard and soft, hot and cold, and all within a microsecond. If she could get him into a middling mood, she would call that a win. The game formed in Clara's mind. She felt too good right now to deny herself.

But he was still turned away from her.

"I hope you're able to give me kids."

She desperately wanted to move her fingers over her abdomen like he had... but didn't dare.

He still didn't answer or respond, and Clara figured he wouldn't have to as sleep dug its claws in, pulling her under and ending the game before it even began. Her eyelids grew heavy and she closed them.

"We'll see."

She pried them back open and Reid's dark gaze filled her vision again as he leaned over her.

"Sleep now. Rest." His voice was deep and smooth and commanding. Clara gave in without a thought and greedily dove deep into the black abyss of oblivion, an endless pool that resembled his gaze.

* * * *

WHEN SHE WOKE AGAIN sometime later, she was back in her room and didn't feel nearly as good as she had the first time.

She was far too lucid to be happy. Looking across the bed where the time was displayed, it read early morning.

Clara stretched her body, and only minor aches and a weak bout of nausea made themselves known. Her stomach also felt tight.

She leaned up on her arms to inspect it but caught sight of the metal dog curled up in a half donut at the end of her bed. It was watching her in the low light, its jaw resting on its front paws; it was as still as a stone gargoyle on an ancient monument. *Hopefully just as protective, too?*

Her companion had never looked more adorable and less threatening. Gingerly shifting on the bed, she curled up in front and laid her head down on the mattress facing it. The dog's head lifted slightly before settling back down.

"I love dogs." Clara slid her fingers over its head. If she could never have children, she would adopt a bunch of cats and dogs.

The canine looked at her lazily and without emotion; it didn't stop her from loving it. She continued to pet the metal-plated skin over its neck and back while her other hand reached out and cupped her curved belly. She could feel the remaining glue that held her incisions together and the bizarre tautness that it provided.

For the first time in years, she finally felt whole. It felt like her fairy godmother had finally granted her most fervent wish. Right below her hand was the first step in taking back control of her life.

She was determined to be pregnant by the end of this day.

Clara grumbled and sank into the bedding.

"I'm glad you're here with me," she said softly. The dog had no reaction and she sighed sadly to herself. "No one's ever been there for me. Not in any way that matters. Not without expecting something in return."

Stop wallowing. Today's going to be a good day. She closed her eyes and allowed herself the luxury of waking up properly.

She didn't know how much time had passed, but when she sat up later she was more awake and the smalls aches she had earlier were gone. When her feet touched the ground, the world didn't spin. That was a good sign—or maybe it wasn't. She wasn't a doctor, but she sure as hell wasn't going to ask her doctor.

Her body was somewhat steady; she knew that much. *At least I'm on the other side of the procedure.*

As she rose the rest of the way to her feet, her companion jumped off the bed and went to her side. It pressed its head into her open hand and helped her balance.

"Thank you," she said, smiling as it escorted her to the bathroom. When her fingers clutched the doorknob, it sat back.

"I'll be right out," she told it before she closed the door and showered.

Clara grabbed a wet towel and soaped up her body, making sure to be careful around the incisions. Faint scars remained from her past but no new ones would form. Even now where her skin was pink, the cuts that had opened her up were almost invisible. When they healed, they would only be a memory.

Those would've been scars she wouldn't be embarrassed about, like a tattoo commemorating her rebirth onto a new path. She frowned at the thought and looked down at herself, at all of her curves, and wondered if a man like Reid could ever find her attractive. She wasn't toned or slender like many of the women that she usually encountered outside the facility.

Growing up, Clara refused to take the body enhancements that regulated the human system. She liked the body she was in, even if others found it odd that she did. It was hers and hers alone.

Santino had tried to take that from her, thoroughly and invasively. Even now she fought every single day to regain what he had robbed from her.

Clara curled her hands over the basin and squeezed the metal, squeezing the hollow pain of her past out with it. Looking at her reflection only reminded her of the features that had caught Santino's notice all those years ago.

I'd been born with pretty eyes and soft innocence. She never saw that innocence but her ex liked to make a big deal out of it whenever he felt like taking it away. And he took it all away.

Back in the foster care system, Santino had burst into her life like a bomb, and she had no protection against such weapons. Clara had caught his notice on the street one day, and he drew her in like a starving kid seeking affection, literally. He shaped her into his little shadow and she grew addicted to the security he gave her... and his twisted control.

Even now she craved it, in the deepest parts of her soul, she was attracted to the dominance he had over her. But Santino's image filled her with disgust, and whenever she fantasized about losing control, the pain returned to her scars. Where he stabbed the life straight out of her.

She dropped the washcloth into the basin and watched the soapy water get sucked down into the drain.

You don't own me now. She looked at the incision and the straight line it made through several of her scars. Reid gave back some of what Santino had stolen. Her heart thumped.

Clara wouldn't admit that she wanted the doctor, nor acknowledge the thoughts that kept inserting themselves in her head about their situation. Cyborg breeding facility. Breed with a Cyborg? Interesting. *Interested.* Stop! That line of thought was enough to summon dozens of scenarios, and each of them ended with her naked and Reid sliding deep inside her.

She squeezed her legs together and tried to deny her arousal.

I always fall for the wrong men. And even the right ones end up being wrong. Clara tried not to think about her ex-fiancé.

She spread a towel on the floor, sat on it and spread her legs, telling herself the entire time that it was simply pent up sexual frustration. That having an orgasm would clear her head and solve all of her problems.

She ran her fingers through her sex, already silken and slippery. The small thatch of curls that she maintained at the apex of her groin was still damp from bathing. It only served to heighten the sensation and the pressure between her thighs. Clara lay back and found her clit, thrumming it with her thumb as her fingers moved in sync inside her.

The sensations grew, but so did the frustration. She thought about *him* and the heat of his hand on her torso, his long, precise fingers that had made her whole.

She imagined lying on the medical pod with her legs spread and his fingers sliding into her, where one moment he was professional, and the next he was probing her, playing at being a doctor. Forcing her to submit to him and no one else. Dark light and piercing eyes filled her head.

Clara pressed her fingers deeper in and found the sensitive wrinkle; a hungry moan left her lips.

Her orgasm came out of nowhere and her body shook, feeling every shockwave zing her nerves. She thrust her hips into the air and twitched against each pulse. Her head shook from side to side as the sensations took over. Her hand was soaked, her legs were wet, and the perfume of her arousal and sweat hit her nose. It was fast and perfect and just how she liked it.

As she came down from the high... there were only two things left on her mind.

One, that she would have to bathe herself again, and two, she didn't want artificial sperm in her.

She wanted Reid's.

* * * *

REID PANTED ON THE other side of the door.

He heard and smelled everything and it drove him into a rut.

He barely contained his canine form as he walked back and forth across the room, listening to her shaking breath and smelling the ascending arousal. He couldn't feel sexual desire while he was fully shifted and he thanked the nano gods for that, because just knowing what was happening was killing his control.

I really want to fuck her.

What happened before her surgery was one thing—a lesser thing than what was happening now. If Clara was his and he was a man... Reid shook his head. He would be with her in that room now, pressing her into the ground and taking her pleasure for his own. His jaw slackened, revealing his sharp metal teeth as he tasted the air.

I need to fuck her.

She was on his tongue and in his nose.

Reid eyed the door and debated leaving, but to do so would mean he would have to shift. Or let Clara know that her android dog could open doors. Instead, he sprawled himself out on the bed, maintaining his form.

What had he been thinking? Coming into her bedroom and watching over her during the night. What was wrong with him? He hated his instincts, and he hated the pull he felt for the girl who had forced herself into his life. How could he deny her when everything about her was so appealing to him?

He had encountered hundreds of attractive women in his life, but that was all they were. A pretty face, a pretty body. None of them had the alluring violet eyes that ensnared him nor the smell of tart berries, fresh off the vine, ready to be enjoyed. None of them had possessed such open vulnerability and determined strength.

None of them had every attribute that he seemed to have been searching for, even those he did not know existed. He had never felt such magnetism.

Reid was always in control. Always. That was his mantra, but right now that control was slipping by the second.

He had let his beast get the better of him, and because of it, he was trapped in this room smelling her need barely a few yards away. The need he was ready, able and willing to fulfill.

There was no way Clara would ever forgive him if she ever found out that he was more than a mere Cyborg; that he was also the dog she had been spilling her secrets to, encroaching on her privacy and invading her space.

Sleeping in her bed.

He growled and jumped off. Focusing on his need to get away before he lost it, he shifted, naked as the day he was created and managed to walk away. His disgust with himself lingered as he stormed into his office, suited up and hid a gun in the lapels of his suit jacket.

That disgust stayed with him as his lips peeled back, baring his teeth and as he approached the locked garage at the back of the facility and entered his personal flyer.

That disgust stayed with him as he flew to Pecos, Texas with the cop's phone in his hand, until he traced the source of its last call and ended up at the front of a dilapidated house.

Clara could have her orgasm, and he could have his peace.

Chapter Eight

• • • •

Reid stepped out of his flyer as the angel of destruction, with absolute clarity of his purpose.

He straightened out his suit, cracked his neck and narrowed his eyes. No one could hide from him. He was built for this. The street he was on was all but deserted and the remaining structures had seen better days—better centuries, even.

Gravel and dead grass crunched beneath his feet as he walked up to the front door. Reused metal, modified wood, and cement were the building materials of yesteryear. Wooden resources were scarce and when the world was fighting a war, infrastructure took a beating.

He scanned the interior and found two life forms inside. Both were in stasis, and only the subtle shifts of breathing and the heat their bodies produced suggested they were even alive.

Reid glanced down at the phone clenched his fist and let the shattered remains fall at his feet. The clacking sounds were soft to his ears. Even if he were discovered, it wouldn't change their fates in the slightest, but he didn't want to make a whole day of this.

He burst through the door, allowing the resounding crash to announce his presence as pieces of the doorframe scattered into the hallway. His eyes flashed as one of the lifeforms further in the house bolted upright.

Reid steadily walked toward his target.

A voice yelled down the hallway and he could hear the smooth sound of oiled metal sliding against metal. "What the fuck! Who the fuck are you?"

Reid ignored the ramshackle security feed and the taunts of the man he hoped was Santino. This was almost too easy.

"Fucking idiot! I have a gun!"

The man accentuated his point by appearing at the end of the hall, head ducked around the corner and shooting at him. Reid stopped and waited as every single one of the bullets missed him. Desperation and shock were not the keys to good aim.

Underneath the sound of gunfire and curses, he could hear the murmur and whimpering of fear. The second figure remained still in the room behind the man who fired at him.

Reid cocked his head, hearing the telltale signs of rope. She must be bound. *That would be Marsha's woman, I imagine.*

He surged forward and turned the corner, throwing the man who was frantically trying to load a new clip backward and to the ground. Fresh sweat and fear filled his nose, mixed in with the stench of stale urine and cheap alcohol. It twitched with disgust as the shooter fumbled away from him and aimed his pistol at Reid's chest.

He plucked the gun out of his hand, crushing it before letting it drop on the his greasy head. Placing one foot on the shooter's chest, Reid pressed him down to the floor. It wasn't enough pressure to break a rib. Not yet anyway.

"Santino?"

"Who the fuck are you?"

Reid applied more pressure until the glaze of alcohol vanished from the man's eyes. "Okay, okay, okay! Hold up man."

"Are you Santino?" He hoped not. He couldn't see Clara with a piece scum like this guy, scrawny and haggard and most egregious of all, with bad aim.

"No man, No." The guy gulped under his boot. "I'm nobody, nobody! I'm not Santino. He ain't here. I'm just a hire, a paid hire."

Reid's eyes flashed and it caught the shooter's eyes. They widened with fear as the smell of fresh piss filled the room. *Can't fake that while maintaining eye contact.* Reid sneered down at the miscreant with disgust.

"Where is he?"

"Don't know. I only know he's after revenge. I'm just trying to get paid. Please don't kill me!"

Reid lifted his foot, crouched down and raised the man up by his collar until he dangled in the air in front of him. He threw the husk of his body into the back wall, enjoying the sound of the man's head thumping against it and the way he fell to the floor, unconscious.

He straightened out his suit and approached the fear-stricken woman in the corner. Her eyes were almost as dark as his own. Her hair was a tangled mass around her shoulders and down her back.

He slowly lifted his hands, showing his palms, before he reached toward her face and removed the gag in her mouth.

"Are you here to save me?" Her voice was hoarse.

"Save you? No. I'm here to get you out. The rest is up to you."

She nodded and visibly relaxed as he moved to untie the bonds around her legs and arms. Reid leaned forward and sniffed her hair and she drew away from him as if he punched her.

"They hurt you?" he asked, knowing they had, but didn't know to what extent.

Tears streamed down her face and she looked away. It was enough of an answer for him. Her clothes weren't torn, but that didn't mean anything.

"I'm a doctor." Why he told her, he wasn't sure. The last thing he needed was another woman in his life. "I can help you..."

"My girlfriend—"

"Marsha?" He started by helping her stand.

"You know her? Is she okay?"

He nodded. "She's safe."

"Can you take me to her?" He kept his hand on the woman's arm as he helped her walk out of the room and through the house and into the passenger side of his flyer, where he leaned down and buckled her in.

"You need medical care."

Her nostrils flared as she continued to wipe the tears off of her dirty cheeks. "You don't know what I need. For all I know you could be doing to Marsha what that man did to me."

Reid stepped back and looked at the sky with a sigh as he tried to suppress his anger. The more he offered to help, the more she seemed to distrust him.

This is why I stay away from people. This is why I don't get involved. But then he remembered Clara's violet eyes and his cock stiffened. He remembered the way her arousal smelled as she brought herself to climax feet away from him. *One fucking hour ago.*

He looked back down at the girl in his passenger side seat. "I'll take you to her," he relented.

She sniffled and rubbed her nose. Her eyes remained deadened, staring at her lap. "Thank you."

"Were you raped?" The question startled her but she still didn't look at him.

The woman looked away from him but didn't answer.

Reid gritted his teeth. "Stay here. I'll be right back."

He turned on his heel and stalked back into the house until he stood before the scum trying to get himself off the floor. Before he blubbered out his next words, Reid pulled out his gun and shot him point-blank in the head.

* * * *

HE FOUND CLARA SEVERAL hours later wandering the halls of the facility. She didn't know it was him as he quietly padded up behind her. The cement floors muffled the sounds of his claws. The first thing that hit him was the smell of berries and then her deep, annoyed sighs.

The perfected scent of her arousal early that morning was gone. It brought him relief but it also brought him frustration.

Reid nuzzled her thigh with his snout, startling her, eliciting a drawn in breath, followed by a self-deprecating laugh as she turned and set her eyes on him.

"You."

Yes me. Always me, Clara dear. Reid couldn't resist nuzzling her thigh again and stealing a chaste caress over her jeans. She reached out to run her hands over the smooth metal of his head.

"Where do you keep going off to?"

It was little moments like these that he loved. The companionship, the bubble he created that was only between him and the one other person that had his full attention. These moments were rare and never lasted long, but he savored them.

Clara reached out her hand and he moved forward to sniff it, unable to deny himself, freely reading her emotions. Her scent flooded him with happiness, excitement, anxiety, and a deep-seated contentment. But underneath it all, he smelled the same frustration he currently felt, the kind of frustration that could only be fixed with a good fuck.

She pulled away from him and glanced around. He sat back on his haunches, lazily watching her and happy to do so.

When her eyes met his again, he flashed his with dark light before he could stop himself.

"Do you know... where the doctor is? I don't know your tech..."

Her features swiftly muddled with puzzlement.

Oh, I know where he is...

She continued speaking while her fingers glided over her belly, "I healed faster than I thought was possible. Now I'm at a loss for what I'm supposed to be doing and I can't find him."

His ears twitched, the plated metal shifting in his head. He stood and pushed his snout back into her leg before he traipsed forward. Reid looked back at her in hopes that Clara would follow. She did.

"I guess I'm going to follow you..." she mumbled softly to herself after a self-deprecating laugh.

I'd rather follow you. He shook his head trying to stop those thoughts from forming. He focused on the goal at hand but it became increasingly difficult the longer he stayed in Clara's presence. Or when Clara stayed in his.

They were on the other side of the empty facility, but he didn't take her back to her room; instead, he led her to his office. The door opened as he neared, registered to do so whenever he was close. They moved further into his personal space, where, the night before, he had painstakingly ventilated and cleaned so he wouldn't be haunted by her smell.

Reid bumped his head into the chair across his desk and looked at her. Clara graced him with a beautiful smile before sitting down.

"Thank you." Her eyes darted around, questioning. "I guess I wait here then?"

He barked again and headed toward the door.

"Wait! Please stay with me."

Reid stopped.

"You make me feel safe, protected. I like you nearby." Her voice was barely above a whisper. He closed his eyes in consternation, debating. Reid wanted to stay but he needed to shift back and distance himself from her.

He was about to ignore her plea and head for the door when he heard her rise from her seat and walk across the room. His curiosity won out. Reid turned around and sat, watching her as she invaded his privacy... Like he had with hers.

He looked where she looked and registered what she saw... which was very little. His office was the throne room of his territory and having her in it did things to him. Things he didn't like. First being, he wanted to pin her over his desk and bury himself between her legs. Reid shook himself.

She wouldn't find much, only a few wayward items, as everything about him was embedded in his hardware and coding. And not in reality.

Clara didn't touch anything but as she moved through his space quietly, she was also marking it with her scent. He let loose a growl before he could stop himself. Her eyes shot to his, violet and deep, and with a sheen of guilt.

"Sorry," she gasped lightly as her lips twitched up into a quirky smile. "I won't say anything if you don't."

He canted his head.

"You let me in here without the doctor, so my snooping is as much your fault as it is mine." She laughed but went back to her seat anyway. "Thank you for staying." Her fingers entwined in her lap.

Suddenly, her face softened and her eyes lowered. He measured her, reading every twitch and tremble, every sigh she gave. The weak joy she had experienced before was gone, replaced by something close to melancholy.

Reid padded back to her and laid his head in her lap. It was natural for him. Her hand immediately lifted up to pet the spot between his ears.

"I always wanted a dog, a family. I guess we always want we don't have," she said wistfully. "I've been alone... a product of the foster care system. The sad thing is, my parents are still out there. They didn't die, they just didn't want me. How is that even possible?" Her voice grew husky and her words seeped into his heart. "If I had a kid, I'd cherish them, give them everything I never had. I damn well would make sure they knew they were loved every day of their life."

He smelled the tears before she removed her hand to wipe them from her eyes. Her confession made him sad but also hardened his resolve.

He lifted his head and sat back. When he was first created, he was consumed by one of his basic instincts: the need to lead a pack—to have a pack. And because of that, he would grow attached to anyone and everyone around him in a subconscious effort to create one.

There was no pack mentality among Cyborgs. Those he had bonded with during the war broke apart with the ease of shattering glass as the death count rose each passing day.

Back then, he neither needed nor wanted children. To bring children forth during the war was a crime to him. But now, as he watched Clara, having succumbed to her soft beauty and forceful nature, he could see himself with children—many of them. He could see himself again as the alpha male and Clara as his alpha female.

His fabricated heart raced wildly in his chest.

I could have that. I could have that right now. His eyes darkened again and he was lucky that she wasn't looking at him as they roved over her curvy frame.

She sniffled, wiping tears from her eyes as she leaned back in the chair. He knew he should leave her and come back as Dr. Reid but he didn't want the moment to end.

Clara looked at him and smiled, breaking the haze of his thoughts. "You're a good companion, a good dog."

No, dear, I'm not. You should've heeded the warning.

"I wish Reid would get here," she mumbled. "I just want to get this process over with. I'm ready," she said, saying it with determination. "I hope the process is a good one."

Reid couldn't take it any longer and moved toward the door before she could say another word, leaving before her next damning confession. If he had it his way, the breeding process would be an entirely different one than what protocol dictated. His process would leave her with bruises on her knees.

He barely made it back to his locker room before he shifted. He slammed his fist into the wall over and over again, crushing the stone. It was the only relief he had and he wouldn't take it for granted. Straightening himself out, he dressed in a fresh suit as his last one was covered in blood, and readied to face her.

Reid hoped it would be enough.

Chapter Nine

• • • •

Clara jumped when the door opened. It had been nearly an hour since the dog brought her to Reid's office and as the time lengthened, so did her anxiety.

"Dr. Reid." She stood up and watched as he stormed to the seat behind his desk without looking at her.

Again with the hot and cold?

"You can sit, Ms. Warren."

Clara ran her hands down her shirt, straightening out her clothing before she stiffly sat at his command. She wiggled her toes within her shoes. *I can do this. He's only another obstacle.*

"Yes, sir," she said with not a little bit of taunting. Reid continued eyeing a tablet out of her sight as though he hadn't heard her. The bloody organ in her chest thumped once and she shifted in her seat.

"How are you feeling?"

"Okay. Great actually. I've never had surgery before where I recovered so quickly. Magic?"

"Cybernetics." His cold eyes lifted to hers.

She nodded and vowed not to let him get to her. "Same thing in my book." His gaze narrowed and she quickly added, "I'm ready for the next step." They narrowed further.

"Are you now?"

This time her eyelids slit to match. "Why wouldn't I be? This is what I want more than anything. I want this."

"A child?"

"A family," she retorted.

Reid sat back in his seat. The tablet dropped from his hand and onto the pristine desk. Clara refused to look away as he pursued her from head to toe, ear to ear, and through her skin to the very core of her being. She didn't like how he made her feel, hot and cold all at once, but she wouldn't let him intimidate her.

"Why are you looking at me like that?" she asked after a minute.

"Trying to find the truth."

"I told you the truth!"

His lips crooked up into an annoying smirk. "When are you going to stop lying to me, Ms. Warren?"

Clara sat back, suddenly afraid, unsure of what he meant and where this conversation was going. *This isn't the next step.* She pressed her palms into his thighs. *He's going to drop me. I'm damaged goods. My scars.* A hundred thoughts streamed through her head in a single moment, none of them good. *What if the surgery didn't work?*

When she didn't answer, he answered for her. "Who's Marsha Tannett?"

Clara opened her mouth then promptly closed it. *Why am I not surprised?* "She's a cop helping me with a predicament." *There.* "Can we talk about the next steps?"

"What predicament?" he snapped and leaned forward.

"A small one that's being handled," she shot back in response. "It's none of your business!"

"It became my business the moment you parked your ancient, moldering hovercraft in my parking lot. It was definitely my business when you stepped through the front doors and it was very much my business when you sat your ass in my office and withheld it from me, Ms. Warren. This. Is. Not. A. Fucking. Sanctuary."

Her breath left her but her rising annoyance bubbled into anger. "So that's it?"

His jaw ticked. "What's it?"

"You're kicking me out. This," she waved her hand between them, "is over?" She stood up to leave. If she was fixed, then she could go out and have a child on her own. She'd just have to be immensely more careful. *I don't even know why I thought this would work.*

She made it to the door, her hand on the handle, her heart pounding from her chest, but resolved to let one more disappointment not break her.

The moment she opened the door, it slammed back into place. Clara went still, her eyes wide, staring at the hand that bent a groove into the metal wall. Reid's fingers curled inward until his outstretched hand became a fist.

"Clara."

She licked her lips and didn't move, didn't open her mouth, and tried to stop her heart from beating.

"Sit your ass back down."

Reid removed his hand and the alarming entrapment vanished. She swallowed, memorizing the striations of the bent metal wall, and robotically turned around and sat back down. *He's very strong.* It took everything in her power to raise her eyes to his but he wasn't looking at her. He stood behind his desk, bent over, his fingers spread wide with tension, as though they were the only thing holding him back.

Clara rung her hands and expected to see electrical jolts leave his fingertips.

"Please..." she said at last and he looked at her. He nodded once and lifted his hands away, leaving imprints behind.

"You're not going anywhere, Clara."

She swallowed and squeezed her hands. "Okay."

"Marsha, your predicament handler, came to see me."

"In person...?"

"She came to find you the other day when you were recovering from surgery." Reid sighed, the air about him cooling rapidly. "Her gir—"

"—she made it past all the security?" Clara looked behind her, her eyes darting back over the office, the closed door, and the tall, narrow windows that let in jail bar-like light through half the space. That strange creeping sense ran over her like molasses, the kind of sense she tried to avoid at all costs. *If she made it through... can Santino make it through?*

"She *is* a cop," Reid said dryly. Their eyes met again. "Does her making it through surprise you?"

"No," Clara lied. "But leaving Pecos and traveling through the wastelands does." A thought occurred to her. "Is she still here? Can I talk to her?"

She noticed Reid hadn't moved, not a muscle, a twitch, a fiber, but the color of his irises changed. Sometimes they went dark, shadowy, and it reminded her of the patrol dog that comforted her.

"Later. She's taking *sanctuary* here," he spat the word out. "With her girlfriend. Who was recently being held prisoner by your ex. So she's still here, and I'm now partially responsible for their health, and you, you've become a pain in my tech."

That sense of dread increased as she listened to Reid and replayed his words again in her head. Any excitement about her surgery or the fleeting control she had regained had quickly died. Her gaze shifted back to the windows but it was too bright to see what was outside from where she sat. Clara ran her palm across her stomach, already saying goodbye to the dream she had come here so desperately chasing. There was no way she could have or raise a child while she was being hunted. *I have to take care of* him *first.*

"I'm sorry," she whispered, still searching the windows. "This was a bad idea."

"What do you plan on doing?" It hurt that he didn't deny her stupidity.

Clara pulled herself back in. "I think I'm going to take care of the issue." The thought of seeing her ex again made her sweat in places that shouldn't have sweat. "I was hoping... I was hoping that it would clear itself up all on its own. That when Santino got out of prison..." She stopped and patted her belly. "He did this to me. I'm still surprised I lived through it, but I thought he'd forget about me if he ever got out, I hoped I wouldn't be on his radar anymore, and if I was, I was out of his reach with a new name, living as an extraterrestrial on a colonized planet." Clara raised one of her hands and clasped it over her forearm. "Things never work out, ya know," she laughed humorlessly. "I think I did something horrible in my last life. I must've murdered people, maybe I was a war criminal during the Galactic War, and now I'm paying my karmic debt in this life."

Reid still hadn't moved and it made her feel anxious and comfortable all at once. On one hand, when she chanced a glance at him, he was solitary and focused, but on the other hand, he was intimidating and stern. Hot and fucking cold.

Clara waited for him to call the authorities and have her escorted out of the breeding facility; she waited for a slew of demeaning words to leave his lips. It didn't matter what happened. She'd flow right through it. But the anticipation was what made it hurt.

"Why aren't you on another world?"

His question threw her.

"I couldn't afford it and I wasn't allowed to leave. After the Santino incident, I was in and out of hospitals for years, rehabilitating, and I could never make enough money to pay for transport, let alone transport for a sickly person. The price for my care, to get me safely to one of the outer orbit stations, was beyond what I could make in a year's time."

"There are options."

Why does he care?

"I won't marry a stranger or become a lab rat," she hissed. "Not to get off-world."

"And yet, you seem to have tried both."

Her back stiffened but she kept her mouth shut.

"You had an ex-fiancé, which was fairly recent if what it says here is accurate." He finally moved and pointed at the tablet in his hand. "And when that didn't work out you signed up as the only woman in a cybernetics breeding facility? What about that doesn't say lab rat to you?

"You say you want children, a family, more than anything and yet you're about to throw it all out the window over one man," he laughed harshly and swept his hand toward the windows. The skin on her arms raised. "You're in an endless loop and all because of one bad choice, one mistake. And now you're letting yourself live this way because of it. Santino controls every aspect of your life. Everything. Admit it. If not to me at least to yourself."

"No," she breathed.

"Oh, dear Clara." Reid stood up from his chair and circled around her. She tightened her arms around her middle for protection. "Nothing about your life is yours. Has it ever been?"

He said the words directly behind her; they were breathed somewhere over her hair and into her ear, but she couldn't sense his presence and she couldn't turn around. The prickles on her skin piqued her sensitive flesh, the deep unapologetic baritone of his voice rushed into her, and suddenly she remembered why she couldn't trust men.

She stood and without looking at her lurker, she once again moved toward the door, her hand on the security, waiting for the access to leave. "Let me leave." She needed to get out of his office. Now. Not only because he was an asshole, but because he was just like Santino in that way... that way where she could lose her soul in his presence.

The only difference was that Reid was a doctor, a caregiver, a military veteran who protected the lives of hundreds of thousands of people. He was a Cyborg. And Santino was a street-rat criminal. If she lost her way with her doctor, there would be no running, no hiding, there'd be nothing in the universe that she could do to get away from him. The risk wasn't worth it.

The door immediately swished open. She was sad to find the hallway devoid of her pup.

"This is my choice," she said with feigned bravado. "I'll take care of it and then I'll be back. I. Want. My. Fucking. Family."

• • • •

REID WATCHED HER LEAVE with every wire and piece inside him thrumming with energy. The conversation had not gone the way he had intended it to go. Not in the least.

Her alluring scent overcrowded the four walls of his office, caressing him and filling him with a need to take it and mark it as his. The angry, half-rushed sounds of her footsteps receded into the distance, down the hallway, past the reception, and behind the many doors between him and the living area. He waited until he heard the subtle, damning vibration of her room door closing before he moved back to his desk.

Something in his systems, and in his beast screamed to go after her, for once working in accord without his manipulation, but for his mind, that rooted him to the spot.

Clara was everything he tried not to want in his life. The very thing he avoided. And yet, here she was, filling his nose and his head with everything that eluded him, everything that he craved. She forced him back to his younger self and the need to pack.

Reid cracked his neck and closed his eyes, flushing his systems with clarity. The ventilation went on at his will and began to suck the thick fruity aroma from his space. It wasn't enough; it clung to his suit, and it morphed into a light smell that stayed with him. The air was clean now except for the brief hints, like quiet whispers, or tickling touches on the back of his neck.

He slammed a fist down on the top of his desk, where not long ago he had been playing out his fantasy of having Clara bent over it, and shattered the wooden top.

Santino needed to die. He needed to feel the man's windpipe crush beneath his thumbs, and to hear his last gasping, begging breath before he died. And at that moment, he would loosen his grip, when Santino's mouth fell open on his final, thankful breath, Reid would rip his throat out with his teeth and take that flicker of hope and drown it in torn flesh and blood.

Without a backward glance at his crumbling desk, he stormed out of the office, past the medical lab where Marsha and her girlfriend were staying as they recovered—mentally and physically—through the security doors and straight for Clara's room.

He was going to take something from Santino today. He was going to take something from Santino every day until his existence was nothing but a bad memory in a nearly forgotten dream.

Reid didn't wait for the door to open, slamming the panel into the wall and forcing his way in. His eyes landed on Clara as she jumped back from the open duffle-bag on her bed and the few items she had left to pack.

"Reid!" Her back hit the wall opposite him. He closed the space. "What're you doing?"

The damning scent of her drowned him. He boxed her in, searching her wide eyes, noticing the flare of her nostrils, the dishevelment of her blonde hair. His eyes flashed with dark light as they moved over her soft, pale features.

"You forgot something, Ms. Warren." He breathed her in and groaned. *She smells exciting.* The smell excited him. Her hands hit his chest. His metal shifted beneath, and his dick rose in response. Clara pushed at him but he was an immovable wall. His lips quirked up. *I'm going to take everything, Santino.*

And then I'm going to sink my teeth through your jugular.

"I didn't forget anything." Clara's piercing violet eyes battled his.

Reid leaned in and stared straight into them. "Remember this," he demanded until he got the searching response he was looking for out of her. The moment was forever embedded in his drives. "We're going to make a baby."

He gripped the back of her head and slammed his mouth down on hers, taking the breath she didn't have time to release. It was a small start—but he had time.

Chapter Ten

• • • •

C lara clawed at him, nails digging in and fighting to tear the black-as-death professional suit off his chest. The need to draw his blood and feel it under her fingertips was the only thing she wanted. Adrenaline surged through her to battle him off and get away.

Reid pushed her up the cold, facility wall, and kicked her legs apart, placing his thigh and knee between them, and pressing right into her clit. His tongue did the same thing to her lips, breaking her barriers open and taking over. She struggled against him, to get away from him, but every little space she had to move was quickly cut off by a wall.

"No!" she squeaked and bit down on his tongue, but his hand had captured her head and his body pinned her. Her word was ignored. She kept saying it again and again, even after he rubbed his entire body over hers in rhythm with his tongue and the thigh between her legs. Her fingernails dug into his coat.

Hot and cold. She hated it. Hated him. But wanted him so fucking much it hurt.

The first thing she realized when she stopped fighting and started swaying with his dry-rubbing dance, was what was happening. That her horribly intimidating doctor, her controlling supervisor, was trying to consume her. Because that was what this was. *He's lost his mind.* It made it easier for her to do the same.

The hand that held her head tilted it to the side harshly. His mouth left hers to run the tip of his nose over her raw lips then up the side of her exposed neck until it ended up behind her ear and at her hairline. Clara lifted her dangling, tip-toed feet off the ground and hooked them around his middle. Reid used his free hand to heft her up on him and trap his burgeoning erection between their bodies.

"No," she said, straining up again, more to convince herself than him. "I can't let you consume me." The last part came out as a plea.

He lifted his nose from her ear and stared back into her eyes. This time the annoying rush of budding tears blurred her vision. "Remember this, dear Clara."

"Why?"

She couldn't see his lips, poised a hairsbreadth from hers. Their words created tiny kisses between them. It was too hot, too kind—too much for her. *He's going to go cold on me now.* Clara didn't think she could bear it if he did.

"Because I'm going to give you everything you want," he said, so low she wasn't sure she heard him.

"And if I want to leave?"

The soft brushes of his lips shattered her. "I'm going to follow."

It scared the crap out of her.

"I'm always going to follow your scent."

Clara gripped his shoulders as he pressed her back into the hard wall. Her body tensed and her heart raced while the Cyborg laid down the law.

"Santino is as good as dead—

"—what?—"

—and your body now belongs to me."

"What?" The hazy heat went lukewarm. Reid pulled away and her legs dropped, her feet weakly touched the ground.

"You forgot one important thing, Clara." He moved away from her and the space he created made her feel even more exposed than when she was being prepped for surgery. "The facility owns the surgery, your body for the next three months, and the baby we're going to make. I own it."

What was lukewarm went to cold. The desperate shocks of lust continued to stab holes through her. "I refuse!"

Her eyes followed his deft fingers as they loosened the cuffs of his suit, the one she barely managed to rumple, and she watched as he exposed his wrists. She only stood straight because the wall at her back forced her to. A knotted pressure tightened her pussy.

Reid breathed in deeply, and she knew he smelled it. He worked his coat off smoothly, and any signs of the desperation he unleashed on her minutes ago was gone.

"Don't get undressed," she said. He shrugged out of the blazer in one move, catching it on his fingers, and turning to the one chair in her room to throw it over it. "I'm—this isn't happening? I'm leaving. I'm supposed to choose the sperm? In a lab? This isn't part of the contract," she was rambling, her tongue thick and tied and she knew it. "I'm not supposed to have a real father for my children."

Reid ignored her and rolled his neck like he did often, drawing her eyes as it always did to land on the thick curves of his Adam's apple, the veins, and the almost invisible hint of facial hair. Clara backed up toward the corner and where the side of her bed met the wall, moving to climb over it and toward the door he blocked. He watched her the entire time, steadily, and without emotion.

"Clara." His voice was laced with warning.

Her feet hit the other side of her bed and she stopped. For some reason, she didn't really want to make it to the door, didn't want to escape. She didn't want her hand to leave the bed, not when her doctor watched her like a flower he wanted to pluck or prey he wanted to fell.

"I can't do this with you." She forced herself to step away from the bed. "This'll complicate everything. Everything." She indicated them and the bed. The idea of it all. Clara shivered. It made her want to give in and lie down on the bed like a willing sacrifice. "Go ahead, kill Santino, make it long and painful. I'll stay here and follow the terms of my contract. But we both know this won't work. I'm never going to be with a man again. And if you impregnate me instead...instead of other, safer seed, I won't just have to share my child with the government, I'd have to share him with you too." The stupid tears she wanted to curse to hell reappeared to glaze her eyes as she spoke. Her heart felt like it was in her mouth.

His eyes flashed that familiar dark light that reminded her of the dog. Clara glanced at the door, wishing it was with her.

Reid stepped away from her and moved toward the door. "Follow me, then," his said stiffly, taking her by surprise.

He waited for her, and she dared one last look at her open bag, so close to being packed, before she swallowed and left the room with him. He took her arm, his heavy fingers reigniting her need, and led her back to the same medical lab where he had reconstructed her womb.

The air was chillier than the rest of the facility and as Reid ushered her in and powered on the tech, he appeared right at home. Clara wasn't sure what to do, disheartened, sad, nervous, even scared, scared that she condemned her ex to death by this Cyborg without a guilty thought.

Her body was flushed with desire, her pussy still clenched, searching for something to fill it. Her eyes landed on Reid's back where his white button-down shirt clung to him. That prospect had passed and what was between them now was strained and growing icier by the minute.

She frowned. It was as if the whole day had never happened. *We never talked about my predicaments, I never waited for him in his office, Marsha and her girlfriend aren't here. We never kissed. I never felt his massive erection.*

Reid indicated the pod, now shaped back into a slat, for her to sit. Clara rubbed her arms and for the second time that day, she sat her ass down where he told her to.

He hadn't bothered putting on a lab coat as he stood before her, handing her a thin glass and metal box with a tablet screen on top. "These are your choices."

Clara glanced at them, not reading any of the descriptions, before shoving it back into his hands. "Okay."

"You don't want to look at them?" he asked, amusement in his tone, and canted his head.

"No. The first one. My kid is going to be perfect no matter what. It doesn't matter what super cyber DNA he has, he's mine." She didn't mention how much she didn't want to have this conversation with him. Not after what had just happened and especially not now that his erection remained visible and was almost at eye level with her.

"All right," he chuckled and picked something from the box at random. She closed her eyes tightly against her budding curiosity.

This is it.

Reid turned away and plopped the tube he held into a machine. The slight clink and the buzzing receptacle made everything there was between them nerve-shatteringly clinical.

When he turned back toward her, he looked at her strangely.

"The sperm you chose—"

"I don't want to know." She made a face, looking everywhere but at the elephant in the room and his hard-on.

"Has cellular technology for enhanced senses."

Clara frowned and his smile widened.

"Your son will be born with perfect sight, smell, hearing, touch, and taste. But then again," he lifted his shoulder, "all the sperm in that box does that. Would you like to know more?"

Bastard baited me.

He moved to her side and adjusted her seat to tip back, the bottom raised, and pushed at her hips, while the rest shifted until she was making a shallow U-shape, knees still bent and lower legs hanging off the end. She took a deep breath and refused the let the position make her feel vulnerable.

Because she was damningly vulnerable.

"He'll be healthy for life and strong, that's all I need to know. He'll be a bipedal human being and have a long life. An education that others would kill for and a mother who loves him more than anything in this universe and the next. He'll have a family."

"Hmm." Reid rubbed his thumb over his lower lip, bringing back his talking kisses to the forefront of her mind. "He's lucky. Generally, cybernetic beings don't have families."

His face shifted and he looked sad, haunted for a moment, but then it was gone. She wondered if his childhood was like hers. *No. It was worse. He didn't have a childhood.*

"Maybe they should," she said without thinking.

"Maybe now, but during wartime, no. Having a family was a nightmare. The kind you can't wake up from."

She reached out and grabbed his hand, squeezing it. "It's not wartime anymore, Reid. Hasn't been—"

"—For forty-three years, eighteen days, twelve hours, and sixteen minutes since Lysander ended it. Still feels like yesterday."

Clara never heard of this Lysander. She remembered learning about that final battle where the Trentian colony ship, filled with hundreds-of-thousands of aliens had exploded, blipped from existence. There was no video of it, no feed, only that the location of the event was classified and that those who knew where it had happened, said not even rubble remained. The Cyborgs caused it. The survivors, the only ones, those Cyborgs, still lived.

"Were you there?"

She let go of his hand but he kept it trapped.

"No."

"Was he your family?"

Reid laughed again. "I don't have any family."

"Me neither." Clara peeled her eyes from him, the tension between them growing too heavy for her to handle. She settled back instead. "I'm ready."

He let go of her hand. "Are you now?" Reid was taunting, teasing her. "You're going to have to take off your pants."

She closed her eyes and sighed, again. Then she opened them and looked directly at her doctor's dick before shuffling up and pulling down her jeans, her shoes, and leaving them in a pile at her feet. "Can I keep my underwear on?"

"Hmm." Reid blatantly checked her out.

"I hate you." *Why are you a rollercoaster in a man-suit?* But the way his eyes followed every curve and groove of her body, as if memorizing it, dispersed some of the chill in the air.

Knowing they could be naked and thrashing on her bed right now didn't help at all. Clara didn't wait for him to answer before positioning herself back in the chair.

The machine with the sperm stopped vibrating. He went over to it and took the tubular contraption out before returning to her side.

"You don't hate me," he said while rolling the tube between his fingers, making her eyes follow its movement. "This sperm was taken from a Cyborg before he awakened, stolen and labeled anonymously, in a way that can't be traced back to him without being in direct contact." Reid handed it to her. The container was cold to the touch.

"We don't have rights until our central nervous system, our organics, are paired with our nanocells and our pre-created internal technology. Once that first connection is made, we have rights, but until then... This one..." he tapped the side of the tube with a finger as she stared at it. "Has a singular cellular strain of nanocells, ones with reflective properties, almost like a mirroring effect.

"Although your son will be human, he'll be able to change the transparency of his body in minor ways. He'll be able to change the sound of his voice to mimic another perfectly—if trained—his eye color, hair color, and length, he'll even be able to change the way he smells. Depending on how strong he is and how much of you is in him versus the nanocells, he may be able to change more."

Clara's stomach sank and Reid snatched the tube out of her fingers. Suddenly this felt wrong. Everything was wrong.

And he was smiling at her like a bastard.

"Let's get you pregnant," he said before she could respond. The slat she sat on lengthened at her feet and pulled them apart, lifting them in the air. A band snaked out to clasp her feet. The back of her chair lowered further and she had to fight to remain sitting up.

"Wait!"

Reid ignored her and swiped a series of numbers at the control panel of her interchangeable pod. The machine took the tube from him and it disappeared into the confines of the chair.

Clara slipped her feet from the confines and scurried from the moving tech around her. "This isn't right!"

Suddenly there were arms around her. Warm hands gripped her skin and pressed her back into the seat. A hot breath brushed over her temple and she was trapped back into the chair with Reid leaning over her.

The smell of metal and iron blood, sanitizer, and antiseptics filled her nose, along with the wave of heat that flowed over her skin, banishing the chill. His heat. Her stomach pulled and tugged. So much warmth pooled between her legs. Her fingers pulled at his shirt and met the unrelenting wall of his flesh beneath.

The room remained frigid and he grew hotter, his dark eyes searching hers, his heavy breaths sucking her in, and his lips frustratingly too far away from her skin. One hand curled around her neck while the other was out of her sight.

Neither one of them moved, locked in position, staring at each other. She read him and he did the same to her. Clara didn't know how much she could handle today.

"Is this right?" he rasped out at last, goading her.

She shook her head. "No."

Reid leaned back, his smirk back in place, and pulled at the nape of his shirt. With one hand still curled around her neck, he unbuttoned it slowly. His fingers kneaded the tension from her neck while the other revealed the muscled chest previously hidden. When he was midway, he stopped and stared at her.

She reached over and tugged the bottom of it out of his pants.

And when his chest was revealed in its fabricated and inhumanly perfect glory, she pulled at the sleeves until his shirt was gone.

"Lie back." His voice was hard, pulling her eyes from his abs. "And slip your feet back into the harnesses."

She lay back and did just that, closing her eyes as he moved between her spread legs—legs that spread wider as the machine shifted to allow him to press closer. Clara bunched her hands within the cloth of her shirt, over her scarred stomach, nervous.

His finger slid over her panties with enough pressure to jerk her hips into the air. The next moment, his arm clamped her waist to the seat, her legs went wider, and his singular torment continued. She wrenched her eyes shut, half-mortified but aroused beyond belief.

If I can pretend this is a fantasy... But Reid rubbed the pad of his thumb up and down her again, applying enough pressure that the soft material creased, and she forgot how to breathe without making her body squirm.

"Relax." His voice filled her ears and Clara swore she could feel his warm breath over her clit through her panties. She was sure of it as he began to pant. The heat of it curled her toes. Her eyes shot open. The medical machinery that littered the room outside her bubble hummed with life. The lights they gave off, red, blue, and green, were in stark contrast to the clinical white of the room and the spotlight above her.

"Clara, relax."

Her hips jumped in response. "I'm nervous."

His face lifted from between her legs but his finger continued to pet her in teasing strokes. Reid's free hand tilted her chin and forced her to look at him.

"Is it because I'm going to fuck you?"

She shivered and squeaked out a nonsensical reply.

"Or?" He left the word hanging with a panty-wetting smirk.

Clara shook her head, hating the blush that burned her cheeks that his gaze trailed across.

"Or because I'm going to do it while playing doctor?"

The embarrassment she felt made her want to die. She pushed at his shoulders as he laughed at her.

"I don't think I can do this!" she squeaked, jerking her head from his grip. She sat up, looking for a bed.

In the next moment, the chair dropped back into a pallet, knocking her flat onto her back. Strong hands pushed her into the cushiony material before taking the collar of her shirt and ripping it down the middle. The material was in shreds on either side of her before she could object.

"Relax, Clara," he snickered as he pulled her bra down to expose her nipples. His hips ground between her thighs, pressing the hard outline of his erection into the crease of her panties where his finger had played moments before.

"Asshole," she groaned out when he curved his hands over her breasts, squeezing and simultaneously pressing his cock right where they both wanted it to go.

"Never said I wasn't. Let's see if you're ready?" He ground his hips into her once more before pulling back. The loss of his body and his heat was sudden and had her leaning up on her elbows, searching, finding him between her parted thighs thumbing the belt buckle at his waist.

Her eyes drifted over him, the way his nostrils flared as if he breathed only to breathe her in, down to his flickering fingers at his waistline. Her stomach jumped in anticipation and she zeroed in, waiting for him to drop his pants.

"I think I'm ready," she gasped out, knowing he toyed with her.

"You think?" Reid canted his head and her eyes were pulled back up to his face. The dark light that had become more and more regular emitted from his pupils. *The dog has the same light in his eyes*— It finally dawned on her why she knew that look.

Clara adjusted and unclasped her bra, letting her breasts spill out. "I do," she goaded back, liking how it affected him, liking how as she let her bra drop onto the floor from the tips of her fingers, his chest heaved and the look on his face went from teasing to hungry.

It made her feel powerful knowing the Cyborg wanted her, knowing that the same guy who intimidated the crap out of her wanted her. The butterflies in her belly didn't stop, but the playing field leveled.

Reid opened the black metal buckle above his groin and pulled his belt from around his waist. Time stopped. The edges dropped to reveal briefs, making her bite back a grunt of irritation.

Suddenly he was over her, pressing her back into the chair and sucking on her neck. His hands roamed and clutched at her curves, squeezing and groping everywhere at once. Clara shivered and rested her head back to expose her neck. He towered over her like a wave, but one that liked to crash into her body again and again.

She dug her nails into his shoulder blades despite his constant movement. One moment his teeth grazed her pulse and licked the back of her ear, and then his mouth was suckling at her nipple.

His speed frightened her, excited her. He was faster than human and she was swept up in it.

When her back bowed, trying to press her swollen nipples against his hard chest, his mouth tasting her lower lip, she pulled her legs free and hooked them around his waist.

"I'm ready!"

Reid's hands gripped her thighs, pulling them off his body. She squirmed and fought him but he was too strong and she quickly gave up.

"There's only one way to find out. I'll have to run a test."

He was standing between her legs again despite her desperation, spreading her legs as wide as they could go, hating her panties all the while. His hold on her tightened and strained her muscles.

"Run the fucking test!"

"It's a delicate procedure. Are you sure?"

Clara held back her retort and lay back, using the pressure of his grip on her to rub her pussy up and down his erection. "Yes... doctor."

"Naughty girl."

She pressed her sex harder against his cock in response.

"Very unprofessional, Clara. Tsk."

He let go of her leg and shoved down his briefs. She stole a look but his erection was partially hidden from her raised hips. Without warning—or too much warning—her wet panties were pushed aside and a large cockhead pressed into her opening. It pushed and probed and stretched her aching pussy in shallow pumps but went no farther.

She grabbed his hips in demand for more but Reid didn't allow for it. "Reid... please," she gasped. "Please!" *I've never begged for sex before in my life.*

"You want this?" he asked, his teasing tone now strained.

"Yes!" She was writhing for it. "It's not enough!"

"Ready to be bred?"

All thought had left her long ago. "Yes," it came out as a whimper.

"By your doctor?" His voice was rough, low, where hers was a desperate opposite.

"Reid, I swear to god, fuck me already or I'm going to scream!"

"Then scream."

He grabbed her thighs again and slammed into her.

Clara screamed.

• • • •

HE PISTONED LIKE A mongrel, slamming into her over and over, his speed increasing with every pump.

Reid squeezed his eyes shut and lifted his face to the ceiling, his fingers clawing up Clara's thighs to hold onto her waist. Tight, hot heat and animalistic need fueled him. Behind the back of his eyelids, he saw her thrashing, her breasts bouncing; it was too much, too fucking much.

"Clara," he growled out, feeling parts of him shifting, feeling his jaw extend, his snout springing forth from its metal brackets, and his incisors demanding him to bow over her and hold her down. Reid shook his head, shook himself back into awareness, and stopped his body from going any further.

Her small, clawed fingers streaked his biceps, up and over his shoulders, and back down to his wrists where they stayed and dug in. Her strangled moans filled his ears as his hold tightened around her waist, and when Clara began to dance beneath him and meet his thrusts, he ground into her and stopped. The cryopod slat vibrated, the screws coming loose from its mount.

"Don't stop," she gasped. He looked at her and bent over her body until his chest covered hers. Her taut nipples rubbed his skin. "Why'd you stop?"

Instead of answering her, Reid buried his nose into her neck and breathed in, filling his nostrils with her scent. His cock twitched and jumped in her tight sheath. Without pulling out, he ground his hips harder in a roiling motion, pumping and claiming her as far and as much as he could.

He smoothed his hand up her side to slip behind her neck and hold her in place. Clara's pulse thrummed under his thumb.

She moaned as he squeezed, his teeth skimming along her jawline.

"You smell so good," he groaned out, his grinding thrusts matched the cadence of his words. "Tart and claimed."

Clara's body writhed beneath him, driving him closer to the brink, his balls clenching to pour his seed—seed he was about to release, coded to seek out what it needed and do its job.

The first sperm he'd release that wasn't programmed to die the moment it left his system.

"I'm close," Clara whimpered.

He turned his face to cover her mouth with his own. He opened his eyes and met her hooded, desperate gaze. His shaft jumped and her sheath clamped down on him.

Reid reared up and withdrew from her body. Before she could utter a sound, he spun her around, yanked her forward, and slammed back into from behind as soon as her feet hit the ground. And with the heart-shaped vision of her ass being pounded, he let his beast free and rutted.

Clara screamed and grabbed the slat, her knuckles white on either side. When his name echoed through the room with pleas and cries, he joined the frenzy with his own grunts.

A stinging bliss melted his core, heating his tech to dangerous levels, and a single bead of sweat drip from his brow.

"Ready?" he sneered and reached around to pinch her clit. Her butt jumped up in answer, her back arched and stiffened. *Yeess.* Clara's body answered his question.

A low, rumbling growl escaped him and he vibrated his finger over her swollen bud, shifted his angle for his cockhead to hit her g-spot. Dozens of years of pressure left him, expelled completely as her body tensed, and when her sweet cunt quivered in submission, his shaft joined her in release.

Cybernetic currents of ejaculate shot out, spurting like a faucet into her and he felt it surround his cock, getting everywhere, and filling her up. Reid pressed his hand into her back and held her firmly into the medical slat, letting his cock spill, expand, and take effect. Clara's body lost all tension and she sagged under the pressure, and soon the scent of her climax eclipsed all other smells in his head.

He continued to roll his hips, spreading his cum throughout, but no longer in a bruising way.

"That was..."

"The best fuck of your life?" he finished for her between his teeth.

"Yes."

Reid knew the moment she was seeded, when his DNA found its goal and took over. A part of him connected to the cyber cell as it morphed with her egg, changing it into something inhuman. Into something that was his. His hand pressed her harder into the bed while he waited for completion. Waited for his claim on her to solidify. The muscles in her back twitched but she didn't fight him, couldn't even if she tried.

When it was over, he roared and released her, streaking his nails down her pale back until his hands cupped her ass and squeezed. His eyes flashed and he saw red, staring at his cock still shallowly pumping into her stretched sheath. *Already ready for me? For more?*

Clara lifted up and looked back at him, eyes wide and frazzled. "Reid?"

He smirked and squeezed her ass one last time before he slipped out. "Success."

She didn't move from her bent-over position as he stepped back and surveyed everything that was now his.

"H-how can you tell?"

"It only takes once." He grinned, satisfied, like a young Cyborg who had experienced sex for the first time, finding that it was as good—better—than warring. She frowned and pursed her lips.

When she moved to turn, he stopped her. "Stay!"

"Why?" The questions in her eyes deepened.

"I want to remember you like this. A post mounting from a mutt," he muttered as his eyes left her beautiful violets to look back between her spread legs and the soft, roughly-used quim still in full view. "You're still in heat, aren't you?" he couldn't help himself.

Clara settled on her elbows and brushed her wild hair over her shoulder. A shoulder and side neck that was marked red from his teeth. He briefly reached up and slipped his fingers over his marks and through her tangled strands.

She snorted. "I've never known someone like you. The things you say..."

Reid smirked and kneeled between her legs. When she jerked, he stopped her. "I said. Stay."

"This is embarrassing me!"

"Clara, dear, you just let your doctor rut you so hard into a medical pod that the cushion on top will never be the same again. And this embarrasses you?" He watched fascinated as her whole body trembled and her buttocks and calves tightened. "You are embarrassed." *I like it.* He leaned in and filled his nose with the mixed scents of their sex.

"You would be too if you were in this position!"

"If your face was inches from my cock? Your lips dying to taste it? I don't think so." Her sex clenched and as it did, a bead of excess sperm appeared and trickled out.

"I hate this. I hate this. Stop saying things to make me squirm." But her tone and her body said otherwise. Reid watched his seed continue down her inner thigh until it stopped.

"I like making you squirm." He flicked her clit once and lifted back to feet when she moaned. Before she could stand, he retrieved a cloth and cleaned her up. When he was done—tossing the cloth into hazard waste—he helped her upright and they eyed each other in stifled silence. The room grew chill again and when Clara lifted her arms and covered her breasts, he couldn't hold back his grin.

"Still embarrassed?"

"You're an asshole."

He grabbed her arms and tore them from her chest. With a strangled squeak leaving her lips, he buried his face between her breasts and pressed them together. Reid urged her back onto the pod's edge once more as he suckled and teased, spending the time he should have before worshiping her lush curves. It was almost too easy how quickly she stopped protesting. Too easy when she leaned back onto her hands and allowed him to feast at his leisure. Too easy to bring the strong heady scent of her arousal back. He lavished and nipped her peaks until they were raw, until the color of them matched the color of the marks on her neck.

And when her legs spread for him again, he slipped inside, taking back every delicate inch of her tender flesh.

The rest of that afternoon he made sure he did his job, and that he did it well. And plied Clara with enough of his seed that she'd never be without it again.

Chapter Eleven

• • • •

He left her in his bed, soft and well-loved, the marks of his claiming all over her body.

Reid sat next to her, uncomfortable in the after-throes and with the cuddling, unable to find a position to relax because a niggling sensation of guilt tapped at his gut. He used her. She used him. He gritted his teeth thinking that they were equal in that matter but they weren't. He ran his palm down his face.

Clara had fallen right to sleep as soon as he laid her on his bed—he remained wide awake. The metal in his body longed to release and reform, shift and resettle, to make him back into the canine he was so he could find peace and sleep with his—

With Clara.

His mutt had a better sense of smell, a sense of hearing that was intensified. His beast had a simpler state of mind, an alert one in which he was not bogged down by everything that made him a man... and a machine.

Everything is easier when I'm not human.

Reid shifted his teeth in and out, his claws as well, finding the process moderately relaxing. He kept his back to her, afraid he'd wake her and take her again.

Even now, after everything, after the consumption of her body, submitting to his dominance, and even after he started on the long and tedious trek to claim everything of Clara's—starting with her body and her desires—he was restless, his beast growling to prowl.

Reid gritted his teeth and stopped himself, having already risen from the bed and circled the edges of the room twice.

Restless.

His eyes shot to Clara turning over on his bed, burrowing deeper into his covers. He moved to loom over her vulnerable, sprawled frame and sniffed the hair that lay across his pillows; calculating each of his movements so he wouldn't accidentally touch her.

She won't hear me, smell me, know in any form that I'm here.

Reid read her movements, willed his internal tech to scan and access every part of her at every moment. If Clara awoke, he'd know. If a heavier breath escaped her lips, he'd know. If her foot twitched.... he'd know.

He knew a lot already, almost everything when it came to her physically, but now that she was his and part of his pack—the idea he didn't want to acknowledge because it felt so fleeting—he wanted to know her mind.

His eyes left her face, his nose her ear, and trailed down over her exposed neck, keeping his lips a hairsbreadth from her skin and giving whisper kisses to the messy tendrils of hair that resided there. His heart recalibrated to beat with hers, weak and slumbering. Reid stopped before he nuzzled.

But his fingers trailed up one of the blankets covering her, and gently slid it off her right arm. It was so easy. Clara slept in a prey position, clasping one of his blankets between her arms and legs, lying on her side. Her backside would be exposed if it weren't for the other sheets on his bed. The position did stop him from burrowing his nose between the gap of her breasts but he didn't mind, releasing the need to do so with one quiet groan.

He continued his descent down the run of her elbow, close to her vein, and followed it back up where her fingers were cinched under her chin.

If she wakes up... he wouldn't be able to stop the sudden fear that would crash through her, seeing his face in front of hers. A survival reflex. *I do so like the smell of fear.*

And seeing Clara's violet irises wide and bright, terrorized for an instant before comprehension dawned wouldn't be able to stop him from covering her and taking her again.

She fears Santino, not me.

With the metal wires vibrating behind his teeth, Reid took a heavy step back and eyed her from a safe distance away. There had never been a woman in his den before—nor anyone. Her pale skin and soft curves amongst his sheets brought forth a horrible need to trap this moment for eternity.

The wires strummed harder, practically begging him to shift. He glared at the cement walls, ceiling, and floor on all sides of him, disgusted. There was nothing of comfort, nothing besides his bed.

His suits were hung in a closed, attached closet to the adjoining bathroom which was just as cold and uninviting as the rest. Even the air was cold. The whole damned facility could've been a cross between a mechanical plant and a prison if no one looked hard enough.

Reid paced, his bare feet hitting that cold cement he was coming to dislike. *Can babies tolerate cement? I'm going to have to get a rug.*

There was one piece of furniture in his room besides the bed, and that was a metal nightstand where his hardware was stored, and a gun.

Anything else he *had* was stored elsewhere in the facility. He kept several EMPs stored throughout, smuggled in when he first began working here because he knew one day they would be needed. A Cyborg needed to protect the secret of cybernetic children. The information he kept hidden and the rest that he fabricated would someday be outside the reach of his keeping. He trusted none but another Cyborg with it, and a Cyborg would never take his position willingly.

Seeing Clara in his space filled him with unease. It also filled him with satisfaction.

Reid's lip jerked. He was a mal-crafted anomaly even for his own kind. If anyone was going to make cybernetic humans by natural law—it would be Cyborgs. Not humans.

But until that day of severance came, they'd hide what they knew and continue to work alongside their creators amicably.

"We are, after all, part human too." He checked Clara over once again, obsessively, sensing her REM cycle at its deepest state and moved to redress, trapping the canine further behind a man-suit that then put on another... suit.

When he fixed his tie into place, he allowed one last, lingering breath to fill his nostrils and his memory. Bliss. Berries and seed. Clara's berries buried among and entwined with his smell gave him ownership of it.

He quietly lifted his bedside gun and holstered it behind the lapel of his jacket, keeping his eyes on the woman in his bed the whole time. She mumbled and stretched her half-exposed leg outward, shifting the blanket back to reveal the thin white edges of her scarring.

Santino didn't know he was going to die tonight.

He was filled with a sick sort-of glee.

Clara's words replayed in his head as he walked backwards toward the door. *"Go ahead, kill Santino, make it long and painful."*

Oh, dear Clara, you know how to woo me.

The door zipped open—without a sound—and he stepped back and into the hallway. It closed the same way, hiding her from his eyes. The lock clicked into place loud enough for only him to hear and he turned away. The ventilation system partially cleared his nose, and with it, his head.

Reid found Marsha and her girlfriend, Natalie, several barricaded security doors away and stormed into their room without announcement or hesitance.

They were awake, startled, jumpy in that way only past trauma made a person, but ultimately annoyed by his rudeness.

"Dr. Reid..." Marsha muttered, standing up, back stiff, a show of wary thankfulness flashing over her face.

"Officer." He looked at the other woman, her legs curled into her chest and perched on the bed. "How are you feeling?"

"Better. Much better. Thank you, sir, and—"

"—good—"

"—I'm sorry for being ungrateful before. It's hard to trust easily after... what happened."

Reid nodded.

"We want to do what we can to help with Santino, for Clara, it's personal," Marsha added, her eyes growing harder by the second. "I hate men, no offense. Scum of the Earth."

"None taken." Reid tapped his finger on his lapel, over his gun. "I hate Trentians. We all hate something."

Marsha mumbled in agreement.

He didn't come here to talk to the women, which they understood when he cleared his throat and things went into an awkward territory. He pulled back his sleeve and projected the screen from his tablet from his wrist, the skin on his arm peeling back. The contents filled the space before the two women.

"You're not pregnant."

There was a moment of silence before a horribly stiff exhale passed between Marsha and Natalie. The screen changed to project what medical had uncovered: the inside of Natalie's womb, the obvious health of her reproductive organs and an untouched egg from ovulation. The beginning signs of her next menstrual cycle on the horizon.

"You'll have your monthly within the next few days," He tossed a small vial through the projection to land next to Natalie on the bed. "For your cramps."

"T-thank you." The quickening smell of tears made his nose twitch but they never formed in the woman's eyes, and they never fell.

"You're welcome."

Marsha sighed, saving him from any more emotion, and his projection dropped, his sleeve back in place. "What now?"

"We kill Santino."

"Thank fucking god. What needs to be done?"

• • • •

SEVERAL HOURS LATER, he waited outside the Dallas city limits, standing in the shadows of a slum that was long-ago abandoned. Graffiti graced every wall and surface around him, and what wasn't covered had been corroded with rust on top of rust or crumbled with deterioration where old metal met stone.

The shadows were long and thick in the ancient cities, where only miscreants and the occasional vandal lived, but they were otherwise deserted, taken over by wisps of the past. The old world only held glimpses of what it used to be. It made Reid fidget. Being amongst rotting metal, it made him feel itchy, as if he stood amongst the corrosion long enough, it would take him with it.

He deleted the thoughts that arose in his head and sniffed the air. Even the air here barely held the hint of human inhabitation. Places like this reminded him of how few humans were left, how fewer females still. And even fewer Trentians.

The wait continued and his thoughts roamed. Clara told him how it was impossible to leave Earth because of her medical issues and the debt that arose from them. But it was impossible regardless. Women were detained every which way from going off planet; fertile ones being stranded was no secret the government held. It was harsh, trapped on a sad world.

Commercial cruises and vacations were one thing. Those were allowed to all sexes equally. Women could leave with regulation, knowing that they were forced to return. Women could also leave if it was for an Earthian regulated job—usually contracted for a span of time and impossible to back out of, but a single female, even those attached to families, whether through marriage or blood, had to jump through endless hoops to get off-world.

If a woman wanted to move to Gliese, to Kepler, or to one of the other space stations floating about and wasn't contracted into a governmental position or corporation (one that could pay the fees), it was impossible. If a woman was caught fleeing, it was treason. If a man was caught smuggling women off-world, it was a life sentence on a mining rig or prison planet. If a woman was caught smuggling other women off Earth, well, it was treason and a life sentence.

The news was paid to scare them to stay.

Clara was stuck on Earth. Reid caressed the handle of his gun in thought.

Laws were currently being pushed through to demand all space-born children to travel back to Earth for their education. *A trap.* The technology to create babies from vats was used extensively, but not enough to counteract a century of war.

Even now, female children were being hidden away and raised as boys. Every day the noose tightened because the control slipped a little further away from those in charge.

His systems picked up movement. Marsha was in position with Natalie who was made to look like Clara as bait. The two of them waited at the drop-off point, but time continued to pass and no one showed.

If Santino took the bait, life would be easier, if he didn't—and Reid knew the criminal wasn't any other testosterone-fueled imbecile—they'd have to move on to plan B.

Plan B was both lot messier and wouldn't give Marsha and Natalie the delicious satisfaction of revenge.

He cracked his neck and shifted his canines back and forth, into and out of his gums. Another signal coursed through his sensors, stopping him mid-shift.

Reid brought the intrusion forward, a message, private and secured to all hell-and-back presented itself; it was encrypted and sent directly to his IP address, the type of network message that skipped the normal servers and channels of regular correspondence.

Which meant it was Cyborg mail.

He rescanned his perimeter and checked on the women before decrypting it and downloading the missive into his hardware. No virus was attached, but there never was. The was an easy death sentence to the sender if ever caught.

He preferred to speak to his brethren one-on-one but his curiosity won out.

188.151.3.111. The message was from Rose. *Rose?* *What the fuck?*

She was a doctor, like him, but lived and worked in Ghost City. They communicated once every three to five years, to share new information and developments, but all that was preplanned. She held up her end when it came to cybernetics run by cybernetic beings, and he kept tabs on, well, human experiments on cybernetics and cybernetic beings.

His heart thudded against the metal in his chest and his eyes roved through the heavy shadows and patterns of wall art from eras past. He felt a bottom feeder creature of worry suck at the wires in his gut. This was why he didn't get involved. This was why he remained alone. His need to give all his attention to Marsha and her girlfriend weighed against the abrupt message from a trusted colleague. Reid stepped further into the gloom and made his choice.

Dr. Reid Canis,

First, let me apologize for this message and its inopportune appearance. I hope it finds you at an easy time.

Please delete all traces of it and any sources it's attached to after you're finished reading it.

To get to the point, we have a human female aboard Ghost, attached to a temporary resident, Dommik. She's pregnant.

A bubbling sense of anger rose within him. Cyborgs didn't get females pregnant—ever. The risk was too great. The law of it was well regarded... but in recent years more and more 'borgs ignored it.

Even he ignored it, thinking about Clara, and his seed that had already claimed her egg. He let some of his anger simmer down to frustration. He disliked what he couldn't control.

Every other Cyborg started their family in the security of deep space... if anyone was risking his species, it was him.

He read on...

The fetus is unusual. The pregnancy abnormal. Katalina is well into her second trimester but has shown no signs that she has ever progressed past her first. The child has... Dommik is like you... and with unconventional DNA.

Kat remains bedridden and attached to medical all cycle long. It's stabilizing her and slowing down all progression even further. I'm afraid I may miss something...

Attached is her basic chart—nothing incriminating. They won't be much help, I believe, but it's something at least. Some information I can give you.

My reason for this correspondence should be clear. You should know by now what I want from you. What would benefit our...

Don't send your response. You'll either give me what I want or not.

Rose.

Reid deleted everything immediately, having already memorized everything, before connecting back to the network. He quickly then sourced out all traces of the message through the network for as far as his signal allowed him and cleaned up the trail. He knew Rose would take care of things on her end.

When he grounded his conscious again, his fists were clenched at his sides. He loosed his fingers before he crushed the metal in his hands, straightened the sleeves of his jacket, checked his gun, shifted his canines back and forth once more, and stepped back out into the moonlight.

Dommik was a shifter, like him, but not. He was a hundred times worse. Even now, after dozens of years since their last meeting, he could see Dommik's ropes clogging up the Cyborg's ship, back when they were both commanders. They worked in the same fleet and battlestations as many of the others of their kind—shifters—and no one went into Dommik's territory. Ever.

Not because it bothered the Cyborg and his peculiar tendencies, but because it was private.

Like my den is private. My family. My fucking office and even the damned parking is mine on a good day.

Reid checked on Marsha and Natalie's position, finding no movement on their end, and walked headfirst into the street, over the potholes and broken asphalt, until he got into his flyer and was positioning to land beside them mere minutes later.

The doors shot open and he didn't say anything, didn't need to because his face said it all. The women loaded in and he shot up into the air.

"That sucked," Marsha snapped the safety of her brand new gun, one he replaced before they had left the facility.

"He's not an idiot." Reid really wished Santino was. But the guy left no trail after prison and knew how to keep on the down low.

"Would've been too easy. So now what?" Marsha asked.

He drove them to an open bar, landed, and reopened the doors.

"Get out."

"What? Why? Where are we?"

"Safe. Now get out."

They didn't move and he made a show of eying Marsha's new and very expensive gun. His gaze screamed: I'll break it too if you annoy me. He'd crush it and leave them weaponless before she ever had the chance to fire it.

"We're not moving until you tell us what's happening. We could've waited longer, the night has barely begun, there's hours left to go! You made us fucking leave and owe us something for standing there lamely for nothing. What the hell, Cyborg? Do you even know how to deal with humans?"

Reid sighed, holding back his annoyance. "Plan B doesn't involve you."

"Like hell it does! Santino takes Natalie," her hand came down on her girlfriend's shoulder, "and it's not personal for us because you say so? What has he done to you?" she hissed. "A woman's revenge is one of the only things she has left in this god-forsaken universe."

He held back the flinch her words spurred, hitting home where his thoughts had previously been. His palms ran down his thighs as his body caught up to his tech to stop the pounding that built in his temples. When he commanded people, they listened; when he ordered, questions weren't asked. When problems like Clara arose, like Marsha and Natalie, it made him annoyingly vulnerable.

"Look. Cop. Get a drink. Get several on me." He searched for the right words. "But what's about to happen—with me—won't be pretty or safe."

"I'm trained, Reid. Back up. Ever heard of it? I'll be back-up," Marsha's voice lowered and he knew she noticed the change in him.

The pounding in his head intensified. His canines unlocked in his jaw, demanding to be released.

"I've killed before, I'll kill again. And for a lot less," Marsha said.

"You can't die!"

The silence after his admonishment only ratcheted up the tension coursing through him. The aroma of berries clawed at the back of his senses. The whistle of wind flowing through his flyer, only to escape again, hounded a barely buried need to shift and join its journey. The berries left him and were replaced by the smells of the two women in his vehicle.

"Why?" Natalie broke the silence quietly at his side.

"Because..." Reid glanced at her then at Marsha through the mirror. "Because I know you now." He didn't know how to explain it. How to relay what the canine inside him demanded, what it wanted, what it needed. How to put into words how hard it was to know someone then lose them during war.

The silence was deafening again until Natalie turned away from him, his knuckles turning white over his knee. He watched as she stepped out, as Marsha glared at him through the front window's reflection while she followed her girlfriend. The doors closed and he could breathe again. A knock sounded on the glass next to his head.

Reid lowered it. "What?"

"Money? Drinks are on you, right?" Natalie asked.

For the first time that night, Reid smiled.

Chapter Twelve

· · · ·

C lara woke up sore and stretched her limbs out, fighting
the endless pile of blankets to catalog her aches. Even so,
everything was perfect. *Almost.* Nothing was ever perfect, but
sometimes it got close and right now she was close enough. She
sat up and looked for Reid, her hand emerging from the sheets
to investigate his side of the bed.

She frowned when her hand came across nothing but more
blankets. Her gaze lifted to find the room empty, the bathroom
panel open, and the room beyond dark and empty as well.

She dropped back into the pillows and huffed, reaching
one hand back over to his side, finding it cold.

He's not here and hasn't been here for some time.

She shuffled the fabric away from her and stood up, groaning from the tight pain that flooded through her calves, thighs,
and even her lower back. Clara looked down at her body, expecting the worst. Red marks lined her skin in stark contrast to
her pale body, perfectly sized and shaped to Reid's fingers. She
was marked from toe to shoulder by him.

A whimper escaped her and if she hadn't felt well and truly
fucked, she sure looked like it. The spot between her legs hurt,
but it was a satisfying type of pain.

Clara trailed her fingers over her scars and felt little—not
sadness nor anger—for once, it was the only part of her that
was numb. For once, she had them but they didn't have her.

Her thoughts shifted. She had his seed.

An anxiety-riddled shock of excitement shot through her. Reid told her it only took once. *Once.* That with him it was a one and done kind of deal. It didn't make sense to her why the facility was even open if that were true—open and with a zero-percent success rate.

Maybe because the sperm the cybernetic doctors stole was useless?

Karma?

Thinking about it made her head hurt. She'd only come here for the surgery anyway. The baby—if there happened to be one—was a bonus.

He said it only took once... She tried not to dwell on it as she stared down at herself but it wouldn't go away. *Does it even matter?* If there were secrets to the facility and between Reid and the rest of the world, did she really care? It didn't sit well with her. The elation she felt was marred by it.

Clara ran her fingers through her mussed-up hair and headed to the bathroom, took her time showering—hoping Reid would join her but didn't—then got dressed.

The panel to his room didn't open when she approached it. She stepped back and tried again and it failed to open the second time. She jiggled the handle.

She jiggled it harder. Nothing.

What?

She called out for Reid, loudly, hoping it was a mistake but as the minutes ticked by and there was no answer, she gave up.

Clara refused to think the worst. It wasn't her room after all. Maybe it wasn't coded for her to access. Maybe he was in the lab and didn't realize she was stuck? Maybe he was getting them food? She looked around her for a clock. *How long was I asleep?*

I've been up for an hour...ish? If he stepped out for something quick... he'd be back by now?

The security screen beside the panel didn't respond to her touch or her voice. With defeat wafting off her in waves, she left the door behind to explore.

The giant bed held nothing but a couple hundred blankets (she guessed) and the only piece of furniture was a table beside it with a single drawer. Inside she found a square contraption she'd never seen before and various bits of hardware she assumed was for Reid's internal cybersuit. Touching the pieces did nothing, so she moved on.

There was nothing under the bed except *another* blanket that had been kicked underneath.

The bathroom was standard. Clara was eventually left standing in front of another panel door that didn't open at her approach but when she tried the manual handle, it opened and slid into the wall.

Reid's smell engulfed her even before the door was all the way open. Her nostrils twitched at the worn metal smell of him, which was not as pleasant as when it was coming from its source. Inside were suits, at least a dozen, alone and behind plexiglass. There were no other clothes lining the small space—nothing to get a better read on her Cyborg—nothing but several pairs of matching shoes, ties, and other tech-gear.

On one shelf was a worn dog-collar, with a worn military tag attached to it.

Clara stretched out her fingers, wishing her dog companion was with her, pretending she could feel the strange suede of its skin under her palms. She hadn't seen her friend since everything exploded with Reid, which was odd since it was never far from her side.

Stepping further into the closet revealed nothing else, and it filled her with melancholy. *I have more than he does. I have more and I'm a homeless nomad.*

She had things to her name, items she'd collected throughout her years that she couldn't part ways with and Reid had nothing but the essentials: clothing, toiletries, and a place to sleep. Her fingers slipped down one of the ties, the silk leading their way, and she wondered why Reid was the way he was.

Why did he choose to stay in such a bleak, dead place like this when he had the universe at his disposal? Clara stared at the sleek cloth. He was ageless, powerful, beyond human and yet... she'd never heard of him before. And if he died—would anyone mourn him or care?

I would. She tugged the material once before letting it go and placing her hand on her stomach. *We'd care.*

She crossed her arms over her chest and turned full-circle, taking in everything at once but mostly taking stock of the lack of *everything*. One spin was all she could handle and she moved to leave the closet when a thin indentation—lined into a small square door, almost impossible to discern within the metal framework of the wall—caught her eye. It was cubby-sized, big enough to be the entrance of a crawlspace—or a doggy door—and her hope alighted that it might be another exit if the android dog was Reid's.

She checked behind her and eyed the lighted entryway to the bathroom for a full minute—waiting to be stopped—but when Reid didn't magically appear and nothing happened, she kneeled in front of the square and traced the edges with her fingers.

Hmm...

With a slight bit of pressure, the panel swung inward. Clara tapped it and it swung harder, revealing another space. She lifted the barrier as far as it would go and peered in, her eyes adjusting from the bright closet space to the darkness beyond. Past the gloom was the intermittent LED light of technology and it grew brighter as she moved her hand inside.

She crawled through the door and let the swinging panel rest behind her and at first perusal, she thought she found a hidden server room. Screens appeared and flickered, sensors quietly went off, and the light increased as she moved further in.

The first thing her eyes settled on were the screens, numerous screens, disjointed and placed all over.

She curled her limbs into her body, half afraid that if she touched anything, an alarm would go off or it'd break.

Numbers and codes came next, flooding every surface within her immediate view. She quickly lost interest and stood up, winding her way toward the back and the one large screen that took up the entire wall. Images moved in squares across it as she made her way closer.

Clara recognized it all immediately—the rooms and hallways of the facility. They were from the security feeds all over the building, but as her gaze went from one feed to the next, she discovered they were all feeds of places she frequently visited in the building.

My room. Clara frowned. *From several different angles.* Her throat tightened. She knew what she signed up for and allowed her stomach to settle. She knew she hadn't gone into the situation blindly.

Her eyes moved to some of the other squares that were of the medical labs, the habitable zones, hallways, and the last several, the parking lot. Her eyes roamed over it all again, rubbing her neck. Half the feeds were aimed at her space.

Because I'm the only one here.

Wait.

She scanned all of it again—everything—looking for anything, any movement, but here was no sign of life anywhere in the whole building. No Reid. No Marsha. No androids. And no dog.

Clara tentatively swiped her finger across the glass and it switched the feeds to new angles and new locations. To more *nothing.*

Where did he go? She leaned back on her heels feeling a little betrayed, watching a whole bunch of nothing for no reason, and feeling guilty because she was spying. A little spinning disc at the corner of the glass caught her eye and she touched it, minimizing the security and bringing up a network desktop that was littered with labeled folders in a series of numbers that also meant nothing to her.

She knew she should stop. Something in her gut screamed at her that how the facility was run was none of her business, but her curiosity won out and she looked back at the hidden wall crawl space door one last time, waiting for something to stop her. For him to stop her.

Santino eroded her ability to trust blindly long ago.

And with that thought, she started on the first folder.

* * * *

STILL SOURCING FOR Santino's whereabouts, he found himself at the end of his rope parked back in the empty vestiges of old Dallas again. His spine molded and stiff against the seat-back and while his body was in stasis, his mind traveled the network, clinging onto anything that would give him a lead.

The red flags came first—always. The pieces of information that were public knowledge, that any quick search could find. Santino's imprisonment, his crimes, and the news generated by both.

Deeper in was the information behind the fail-safes, the private info, and the secret sources. Anyone who knew how to hack and hack well could access the deep. Beyond the deep was the abyss, much like the ocean for a Cyborg. That network held its own wonders, and its own monsters.

In the abyss were traces, direct connections with his target, those that went from one IP address to the target, or to an alias attached to the target. That's where he searched now, where his mind roamed.

Reid followed the link from Marsha's phone again and again—the one that led him to Natalie—but there were no more traces to be found. He debated returning to the site and searching manually but discarded it, knowing by now, that whatever he found there would be old news. Santino would have moved on and cut ties.

He sighed in frustration, stretching his limbs, and returning to his body briefly. His eyes sought the moon and found it behind a thick cloud of city-smog. He was pushing too hard and failing. He hated to fail, wanting only to return to Clara with the news her attacker was no more. Time wasn't on his side, though, and he was beginning to regret getting out of bed that evening before and leaving her.

I should never have left—

There!

His mind left his body and flooded back into digital space. He had Santino. And straight from the source, the prison. Leave it to other humans to do his dirty work. Reid experienced a twinge of glee as he started his flyer and shot up into the smog-filled sky.

The target had been arrested. It wouldn't last if he had anything to do with it. Even bars couldn't stop Reid from seeking out his target.

His only problem: Santino had been apprehended on his own turf. In no man's land, in the town nearest the breeding facility. He lifted his gaze to the bleak world around him, and away from the channels of the network. The gears in his cyberware vibrated with anticipation. The night was still middling.

He called up the guard outside his facility, speaking into his wristcon.

"Yes, sir?" No greeting was needed.

"I need you to head to the local station. Bring a weapon and delay any further processing of Santino."

"Sir?"

"It's personal," Reid added, hoping that would answer all further questions. His guard was the only human in his employ and the only one he could stand long-term before Clara.

"This isn't about...? I don't think I can do that right now. There's been a security breach at the facility."

The muscles in his arm tightened uncomfortably and the connection to the guard wavered for a moment. Without a will of his own, he readjusted the route of his flyer, forgetting all about his target. Forgetting everything. Already, his feelers flooded back into his home.

"Sir? Is something wrong?"

Reid's jaw twitched. "Where are you?"

"At my station."

"Where's the breach?" He looked for it as he asked.

"Internal. Unusual activity within the mainframe. I assume it's not because of you?"

Reid felt the red flags as soon as the guard spoke. *Unusual activity*. It was there. How could he have missed it? The vehicle sped up past ground law and went higher, closing the distance between him and Clara.

His world was crumbling in the small confines of his quiet flyer and he experienced something he hadn't truly felt since he was newly created. Dread. So many secrets that were at the tip of a filled dam, waiting to flood over its sides. Secrets he wasn't ready to reveal or deal with—ones he didn't want anyone else to know. Not even her.

"It's not me."

"Do you still want me to go to the station?"

"No. Shut it down. I'll be there soon."

"Do you mean—?"

"Everything."

"Sounds like we're in for some fun," the guard loosed a small laugh and hung up.

His eyes flashed with dark light and his canines popped out his teeth. His eyes zeroed in and searched the wastes for the facility. The old city pollution dissipating behind him. The threads of his suit snapped under the bulging pressure that demanded release.

With his sharp teeth abrading the tissue of his lips, he lifted his wristcon once more, calling into his security room.

"Clara."

He heard her, heard the sudden stiff shift of her body as she was caught trespassing into his space, his fucking territory.

I should've never gotten out of bed.

• • • •

ONE BY ONE SHE OPENED the files on Reid's screentop. At first they led to folders filled with other files and soon she found herself within a labyrinth of layers of data that went on forever. She didn't waste time on anything that she couldn't understand and continued moving on to the next layer or the next folder if only encrypted paperwork or codes showed up.

Every time she opened a new one, she'd glance behind her, waiting for Reid to stop her.

It's been nearly two hours. Her anger at being left locked up in his room, in his facility, without food and completely alone grew with every passing minute. She no longer thought it was a mistake on his part.

The next folder: Reports.

Data. System codes. Programs.

She moved on. It wasn't until she was halfway through that she stumbled upon *him.* Clara shuffled on her feet and sucked in an excited breath as row upon row of images appeared in front of her. Her eyes widened as they took up the entire screen, the entire wall in its mass. The colors vibrant and many. Even in their minimized state, the quality was perfect.

She took a step back knowing she stared at hundreds of memories, possibly thousands, all from Reid's past.

The first image emerged and took over the rest. It was a candid group shot of a bunch of men and one woman decked in battle gear. Nothing about it was clean. There were at least a dozen strangers in motion, some staring straight back at her as if she was living that moment in time. Staring *down* at her.

Clara knew immediately that she was looking through Reid's eyes. Dirt, blood, and grime covered everyone, smoke wafted up from laser-based weapons, some held in limp hands, others clutched with white-knuckled intensity. She'd never seen such haunted eyes. This was war.

The men and women before Reid had recently come back from battle. The filth and grease were evident everywhere.

Is Reid... kneeling?

From that point on, the war images worsened. It was like watching Earth die rapidly before her eyes, the emotions seized her, knowing there was absolutely nothing she could do to stop it. Corpses replaced codes. People replaced programs. The dead replaced the data.

She'd learned more about the war in just a few pictures than she had during countless hours studying it as a kid. It made her problems feel small and insignificant. If there was any innocence left in her that could be lost, it was lost then.

A horrible clarity rushed through her and she couldn't stop the tears streaming down her cheeks, wiping the back of her hand across her face again and again.

When a military image of Reid, not from his eyes lifted before her, she stopped trying to hold back her tears.

The metal image of the dog, her protector, sat in stark contrast against a red background. Reid Canis was tagged, along with other men and metal animals. Her pulse skipped a beat and she stared at her companion, seeing Reid's eyes for the first time, seeing the dog's eyes the same way. The darkness of them. And the black light that they gave off.

Guilt assaulted her and she quickly walked out of the room and into the closet, through the bathroom, and back into the bedroom to pace.

Clara clenched her fists, feeling trapped, wanting to run and scream but knowing there were cement and metal walls that enclosed her from every side. Sweat beaded her forehead, between her breasts, under her arms, *everywhere,* and she rushed back into the bathroom and splashed cool water over her face.

She didn't dare look at her reflection. Didn't dare think of the child growing in her womb. But with that thought, she went back into the closet and approached the dog collar and lifted the military tags attached to it.

Reid's name and military number were embedded on it. The unit he was in and the battleship he was on. *Cyborg* was stated, along with *shifter*.

Mutt.

She took the collar off its stand and brought it back into the main room, staring at it, hoping all its secrets would be revealed to her. And like a good girl, waiting for her heart to stop its marathon, she sat on the hundred-blanket bed and faced the locked panel, waiting for Reid's return. Her stomach growled but she ignored it as she absently massaged the aches from their earlier lovemaking away.

What bothered her was that she wasn't even angry, or scared. Instead, she was sad and numb. Sad for him and the other Cyborgs, but sad for herself too. It was like a big secret had been kept from her her entire life. Clara brought the collar to her nose and breathed Reid in.

"Clara."

His voice startled her, coming from everywhere and nowhere at once. The screen next to the panel lit up and she lowered the collar away from her face, licking her lips.

"Reid?" she squeaked out, her voice raspy to her ears.

"What did you do?"

She was caught, knew she would be at this point, and didn't try to hide it. "I found out... about you."

"You're a liability."

It was harsh and made her flinch. She glanced about for a camera but saw none, remembering the security feeds and having never seen any feeding Reid's rooms.

"What," she swallowed, "do you mean?" *Liability?*

"You not only trespassed into a secure section, but you also tampered with the facility's security, and into its most private data."

"I didn't read the data? I don't understand. It was reports, numbers, and codes... and pictures. I saw pictures from your view. Of you."

The lights around her flickered, making her jump.

"Are you trustworthy, Clara dear?" His voice was so cold. It froze the ice in her veins.

"Of course I am! Reid?" She stood up.

"You're a fucking liar."

"I'm not lying. I don't care about whatever goes on here! But I saw the pictures of you during the war and of your... your other form. I know you're a shifter, a dog, whatever that is being a Cyborg. I'm not lying, I saw it. I looked at the images and I don't care."

When he didn't respond, she wondered if he had heard her. The vacuous, haunting noises of machinery powering down all around filled her ears. The space dimmed to near darkness before she rushed to the bedside table and slipped her hand over the tech until some of it powered on for light. A loud, groaning sound encapsulated her world, the facility's last lingering breath of life.

"You see, Clara, there's a reason I stay alone, live alone, prowl alone. Whenever I get close to someone they either betray me, disappoint me, or die. There hasn't been a breeder here in years, at least not one who originated here, until you. I made a fucking mistake in letting you stay."

"You're being a real asshole!" she shot out into the shadows, her numbness fading and being replaced by confused anger. "I'm not the one who left me trapped in a room for hours with nothing to do but think and explore."

"And prove that you're just another meddlesome girl. Who do you think I'll choose in the end? You or my brethren?"

"Fuck you, Reid."

"Yes. Clara, fuck me."

Something in her snapped, cracked, shattered into an ear-splitting screech of glass through her head. The panel door shot open, releasing her from her temporary prison, to a hallway lined with emergency lights. She didn't waste any time heading to her room, to her mostly packed bag and grabbing her belongings before heading to the reception and the exit.

Reid's office door was open, making her stop and peer in. She suddenly realized his collar still hung from her twisted fingers. Clara slammed it on his desk and walked away.

The early morning blast of the night chill swallowed her up and she hated it. Hated that it reminded her of how cold Reid really was. Hated that he chose to be cold with her.

A dark figure leaned against her flyer door, familiar and cocky, in that way she'd come to expect. Another vehicle was parked next to hers.

"I'm leaving."

"I can tell."

When he didn't move, she rounded to the passenger side and threw it open, putting her bag in the back. She moved to crawl through but was stopped by his foot sinking into the driver's seat. It only stopped for her for a second as she pretended to ignore him and fit her body around it, turning her flyer on and screaming in her head to get the memo.

He grabbed her arm and stopped her from maneuvering it into the air with him still half in it. "What do you think you're doing? You're not leaving."

The piece of her that had broken, now stabbed at her sides and made her bleed. "I so fucking am, you have no idea. If you try and stop me, I think I might try and kill you."

"You're pregnant with my child," his voice lowered and he tried to get her to look at him. Clara gritted her teeth and refused.

"Are you so certain? History says there's a one-hundred percent failure rate at this facility." He winced, and she bit down on her tongue.

"You don't know?"

"I know enough."

"What did you find out?" The hold on her arm loosened slightly.

"That you're like every other man I've ever met. A real dick. Let me go."

"Clara?"

She shoved at him, her hands making contact with the muscled wall of his body and the expensive suit he wore.

"Look." She finally made eye contact with him, her body shaking under the dark light he put her under. The warning *BEWARE OF DOG* rose up like hell's eternal dark gate in her head. "I'm not the liar here. You obviously have issues, issues I can't begin to deal with. And Reid, twenty minutes ago I would've tried. But I can't do this." She shoved at him again. "I can't deal with this hot and cold, freezing and burning emotional rollercoaster you live your life on. I think I could grow up and move on, learn another lesson and adapt, forgive and forget, but you, you can't."

He didn't let her go, instead, he stepped from her seat and back outside her flyer, but his hand held her wrist and held it tight. Clara knew her pulse was beating the pads of his fingers to a pulp. He searched her eyes, her face, and her soul was put under the spotlight of his gaze and she held up under it.

"I'm not the liar, here, Reid, you are." His grip on her tightened but she continued, "I've never lied to you once. Omitted my past, yes, but I never lied. I'm not some meddlesome-fuck-

ing-girl that showed up randomly in your life to ruin it. Sorry
if I had, I truly am but I'm not the one with all the power here.
I've never had any power to begin with. I came here knowing
what I was signing up for." Clara sighed and rested her forehead
against the flyer's manual wheel.

"You're pregnant, regardless of what you say, I can't let you
leave knowing that. You don't understand."

That's all he cares about? All he has to say?

"You know what?" She laughed softly. "After I woke up
from surgery, I was confused why you left all the scarring on my
stomach. I know you could've gotten rid of it like you've gotten rid of the surgical scars. It bothered me but I let it drop. Because, at some point, I stopped feeling them. They were there
and that was it. I felt stronger bearing them. Why did you leave
them? You want me to forget *him*. I know you do."

Clara looked down at herself and the morning shadows
that engulfed her body.

"If I healed them. It would only be cosmetic," His voice was
low and it made her shiver in spite of everything. "I wanted... I
don't know. I wanted to own them," Reid finished on a whisper.
"I wanted you to stop thinking of *him*, but not because I forced
you to."

His answer hurt but she already knew she wouldn't like
whatever answer he'd give her. But it proved her point. Right
from the beginning, she knew what kind of man Reid
was—controlling, dominant, a leader. Like her ex. She gravi-
tated toward him because even though he possessed traits like
Santino, he was still the exact opposite in everything that mattered.

"I'm glad you didn't get rid of them," she said.

"Why?"

"Because they'll always be a reminder of him. I'll never forget him and what he did, nor do I want to. Thank you for your honesty, though."

Reid let go of her as if he were burned.

Clara wasted no time in shutting the door and leaving him behind, leaving the facility behind, passing through the open gates with nothing to stop her. And when she was hundreds of miles away, when her flyer sputtered to a stop well beyond the wastes of America, and she had no more fumes left in her or her vehicle to keep going, she cried.

Chapter Thirteen

• • • •

Clara bent over the sink, exhausted. Water drizzled from a second-hand spout, shooting out in spurts. Watching the resource drain away kicked her into motion g and she washed her hands.

My back aches like a bitch. She stretched, her hands on her lower back, and groaned.

She was showing, like a pumpkin or a marshmallow that was ready to burst in a microwave. It'd only been two months since he found herself stranded in the remains of the Everglade national forest, two months since she took back her life, and yet, she looked and felt like nine months had already gone by.

"Get your white ass back out here, Clara! The night crowd's trickling in!"

"Coming!" She left the bathroom and went back into the dingy bar with its glow of Christmas lights decorated in gruesome waves behind the liquor bottles, placed there by a phantom from the past. Bars would never be a thing of Earth's past. Everybody loved the novelty of drinking in public with strangers. She loved it too. It afforded her a job and one that came with enough tips that would easily save up into a nice security net for her and her baby.

Pregnant women were fun little novelties. And the way she was showing, so quickly and so soon, she was racking it in. A week didn't go by without some drunken proposal for her hand by a stranger, and the regulars had already given up. The bar was going to have a baby. That's how it'd gone down. The men, and even the few women that hung out here had decided in agreement they'd all raise the kid together.

A man in a cargo jacket sat down in front of her, and she smiled. "What'll you have?" When he lifted his face toward the light, her heart stuttered a beat before normalizing. Her smile held.

"You got any scotch? Any Glenlivet? They still sell that around here?"

She turned but watched him out of the corner of her eye. "We don't have that, not anymore... only Wells."

"That'll do."

"Straight?" she asked.

"On the rocks."

"Ice'll cost you. Here it's more than the alcohol itself."

"That's fine. I'm on vacation. I don't give a crap about money."

Clara shrugged and fixed the drink, sliding it to him. Another person walked in at that moment, a regular, one who liked her privacy and sat away and at the other end of the bar.

"So what brings you to this part of the world for vacation? Why not the stars?" she asked.

The man chugged his drink like the world was about to end and she quickly poured him a second before he could ask. Ice and all.

He was handsome, ruggedly so, but screamed military to his very core. They got the military customers sometimes but not often, and not men like this guy.

"I live in space. Lived up there since I was a kid and there's nothing left to see for me there, but I was born right here in the central swamp. A good friend of mine told me to get my feet back on the ground for a while, so here I am, trying to figure out why I listened to her in the first place."

"A lover?" Clara laughed as the guy started in on his second drink.

"More like a sister."

"She sounds like an interesting person, especially if she can sway a man like you."

"Oh she is, and what do you mean? A man like me?" He eyed her over his glass, his lip twitched up in a smile.

"Military. High up, I'm guessing?"

Clara began to feel at ease and moved to the girl at the other end. She handed her the usual soda, kept frozen for her within their precious ice. Her gloved hand reached for it and brought it toward her chest, cupping it quietly. She'd given up trying to talk to the girl weeks ago. Now, she only protected her like the rest of their small community had started to do.

There were rumors. Rumors that she wasn't really human. But no one ever said it out loud, and no one would. Bengie, her boss, supplied the girl with hair dye and contacts and that was all that there was to it.

"You guess right."

She went back to the cargo guy. More customers filtered in. She rubbed her back.

"How high?" she asked.

"As high as I want or willing to go for now," he laughed but looked beyond her to the quiet, hooded girl. Clara stepped between them.

"So we're graced with a celebrity?"

"Only one of the best space pilots in the fleet."

"Is that so?" Clara could do this. Flirt. And with each passing drink she plied the guy, the easier and safer it got having him there. *Third one down.* Several locals watched them from beyond. The door swung open and her eyes lifted away from the game and landed on the one being she'd hoped would never walk in.

Cargo guy kept talking, but she didn't hear him. Not as Reid sat down at his side. The bar went tensely quiet but kept up its nonchalant front. Clara plastered a new, brighter smile on her face.

He watched her like he always did. Like a hawk. Or a very hungry mongrel.

After she'd arrived and stumbled into Bengie's bar, she'd been given a job that same day, and started that very evening. She'd traded her vehicle in and found temporary housing outside the park in a used trailer. It drove, but not in the air, and that was fine with her. On her late nights or double shifts, she was allowed to park it behind the bar, but for the rest of the time, she had a plot of land she rented to buy out in the middle of nowhere.

Then Reid showed up, as a shadow at first and she'd thought she'd gone crazy until she caught a real glimpse of him lurking the perimeter of her home. Once she was sure it was him and not a stray dog, she made it a point to pretend he didn't exist.

Now here he is, in his stupid suit, making it hard to forget him.

"What'll you have?"

"Same as him." His eyes didn't leave hers.

"Ice and all?"

"And all."

Her fake smile faltered. But she made the drink without spilling it and slid it over to him. He haunted her, and she had begun to like his haunting.

"Keep mine coming," military man said.

Reid turned from her, suddenly, and faced him. She went and opened another bottle of the scotch, wondering when it was the last time someone had gone through one so fast, and wishing for a moment that she wasn't pregnant so she could have a drink too.

"You're Chris Anders," Reid said as she turned around.

"And here I was hoping no one would recognize me," he grumbled, slurring his words slightly. The stranger, Chris, faced Reid and frowned. "Another fucking Cyborg? Of course there is. I'm on vacation if you're here to retrieve me."

Clara moved away, needing the space, finding it suddenly hard to breathe and helped some of the other customers out. Bengie tapped her shoulder when she had cleared enough space between her and the men that were making her life a nightmare this evening.

"What's happening?" Bengie asked.

She glanced over at Reid and he was looking right at her. She quickly looked away. "Nothing I can't handle."

"You sure?"

"Yeah."

"Check on the girl. She's acting strange." Clara looked over at their hooded regular, the soda still held tightly between her hands, tension radiating off her in thick waves. And Clara thought her night was going bad.

Oh fucking no. Her eyes widened and she grabbed Bengie's arm and dragged him outside.

"What's wrong? What the hell you doing, Clara?"

"Ben," she hissed and leaned up to whisper in his ear as low as possible. "There's a Cyborg in the bar." Reid was sitting several yards from a complete and utter disaster. Clara wasn't positive, not until that moment, that the girl was a Trentian.

It seemed like an eternity passed by before he got what she was saying and her suspicions were confirmed.

"Get him out of here!"

But he never needed to say it because Reid stormed out the back door, silencing the two of them. The look on his face, cold and hard, and so familiar it hurt her heart.

"Clara," both men said in unison.

I can't with this. But she faced her boss with another fake smile. "Mind if I take a break, Ben? I'll make it up to you, promise." It was so sickeningly sweet it made her teeth ache.

"You sure?" Ben watched Reid like he wanted to stab him through the heart, like a vampire and a Cyborg were the exact same type of bloodsucking monster.

"I'm sure."

When it was just her and Reid again, alone except for the crickets, her fake pleasantries fell away.

"I'm leaving."

It was the last thing she ever expected him to say. Her heart got heavy.

"Why?"

"My brethren need help, elsewhere, and I can't not go to them." His eyes pierced hers but then looked away and down to her baby bump. "Helping them helps us."

"What do you mean? Is that why you came to the bar tonight after all this time?"

He reached out to her but stopped short and dropped his hand to his side. Clara stiffened, waiting, wishing he would touch her, hoping that whatever went through his head would convince him to make the first move.

"Can we go somewhere else to talk?" he asked.

"I can't leave mid-shift."

"Afterward?" the plea in his voice unsettled her.

"Yes. Okay, afterward. But you have to go. You can't stay at the bar." She glanced behind her then back to him. "If you stay, you'll get me in trouble," she lied, hoping it'd take.

"I'll meet you at home then."

Reid lifted his fingers and traced her cheeks without touching them before turning away—without argument—and leaving her standing in the dark alone.

At home.

• • • •

SHE COULDN'T WAIT FOR her shift to be over and as she chugged the scrappy trailer onto her land, Reid was already standing in the middle, waiting for her.

Once again, the bar had survived a near disaster. It was like that every other night. But tonight as she wiped the counters and gave Bengie a big hug goodbye, something in her gut told her she wouldn't be coming back and that she wouldn't see him again.

Clara parked the trailer and opened the door, this time, letting in her stray—as she'd come to think of him— willingly. They sat at a small table in the back.

"I've been waiting, you know," she said, breaking the silence first. "For you to make the first move."

"And you don't call prowling your land and lurking in the shadows not making the first move?" he guffawed.

"No. I hated that."

"You loved it," he countered.

"I didn't."

"You loved every fucking minute of it. It made you feel safe. It gave you space but was a constant reminder that you wouldn't be alone for long."

"You only care about the baby," Clara choked.

"Babies."

She followed his gaze to her belly. "You can't be serious? How can you tell?"

Annoying laughter filled her ears—his laughter. "The same way I knew the moment I got you pregnant. And I am a dog, it only makes sense."

She got up and rushed to the bathroom mirror to look at herself. Reid filled the space behind her. "No way."

"I promise, I'm not lying this time."

His words sobered her. "Good to know. So you're leaving?"

He let her slip by him and move back to the table to sit down. "Yes."

"When?" Did she want to know?

"Today."

* * * *

REID WOULD'VE SLICED off his own hands to touch her but held himself back. Every minute of every day that he followed and watched her, he wanted to touch her. Knowing that he couldn't made it all that much harder. He sat heavily opposite her, soaking up her presence while he could.

She lifted her sad eyes to him. It took him aback and he lifted his lips into a weak smile. "Don't be sad. You're too beautiful when you're sad."

"Where are you going?" Even her voice had grown sad.

"A place called Ghost. A space station where a lot of Cyborgs frequent."

"And it's off-world, off Earth then? Obviously... what am I saying?"

"Yes. As far from Earth as one can go." He pulled at his collar and cracked his neck, watching Clara look out the window and off at nothing. "As far from here as anyone could get..."

Several excruciatingly long minutes went by for him as Clara stared off, the only tell she gave him was the crinkle of her brow. Reid ran his hand over the back of his neck.

When she shifted and looked at him again, a building pressure lifted from his chest.

"What happened to Santino?"

He leaned back, surprised. "So he's what your thinking about when you stare off into space?"

"How else would I think about someone who scares me?" Clara frowned.

"Think about me! Me!" Reid slammed his hand on the table, making it shake. "When someone scares you. Tell *me*, and I'll fix it!" He clenched his teeth, searching for calm. "Santino's gone." And if he had any say—and he did—he would be gone for good.

"Did you kill him?"

"No."

Clara ran her hands over her face, reddening her skin. He wanted to reach across the short distance between them and take her hands away, to clear the wariness in her eyes, to bury his nose behind her ear and into her hair, but he didn't dare; couldn't imagine going back to exile after he had spoken to her again. If touching her sent him back to the yard, he'd ball up his fists and keep his hands to himself.

"Want me to?"

"I thought you may already have..." she shivered. "Nothing has happened since I've been here, nothing," she breathed deeply, "but you."

"I didn't kill him but I made sure the rest of his life will be everything but easy. I—"

"—I don't want to know!" she squeaked out, stopping him. "Save it for a bad day!"

His lips twitched back up into a grin. "So, today isn't bad?"

"Not yet! I don't know..."

Her mouth opened and closed again, again and again. He liked it when she flustered.

"I feel a lot of things right now..."

"I'm sorry," Reid blurted it out before the courage left him. He *was* sorry. He was sorry when she drove away from him two months ago, when he saw nothing but red for the next several days; he was sorry when he finally caught up with Santino and maimed him, deciding to let the fucker live the rest of his life as half a man in a prison system he'd never escape from. Sorry that he hurt her. Reid was a lot of things then but life moved on, and eventually, that life picked him up and took him with it.

She stared at him, her violet eyes sad and wide, and it stabbed him in the heart. The silence killed him.

"I love you," he said.

Tears trickled down her cheeks. Reid watched her cry and when the silence bore on, he mustered up enough courage to catch some of her tears with his fingertips. "You really are beautiful when you cry," he whispered.

"I think it's the pregnancy," she sobbed, dramatically, and the floodgates opened up in full force. "It's not because of you. I'm not crying because of you!"

He snorted, unable to help it, and lifted her from her seat to hold in his arms. The way he wished he had months ago when he had her in his bed—and filled with his seed.

Clara buried her face in his chest as he held her, smelling her delicious scent, made only for him, and petted her hair.

"You really are a horrible, nasty liar," she sniffled out.

"Not anymore. Not when it comes to you."

"How can I believe anything you say?"

"Because I'm going to make it up to you every damn day for the rest of our lives. Even if you don't believe me now, you'll believe me soon."

She lifted her face from his chest and looked up at him. Reid brushed the loose tendrils of her hair behind her ears, relishing the silken feel of it against his skin.

I forgot how much I missed this.

"But you're leaving..."

He caught her chin and pressed his lips to hers. "Come with me," he begged. *Please come with me. I can't be without you. I can't live without my pack.* The press of her swollen belly made his heart skip a beat. Reid knew if he lost her, it would be the end of him. His soul had been broken too many times when he was young; he knew he couldn't go through it again—the solitude, the loneliness, the endless, tormenting need to have someone belong to him, and to belong to another.

No matter how human he looked or how much metal was in his body, he was still a mutt at heart. A dog that wanted a family to protect because they were his. The years had made him into a mongrel, but they had also led him on the path to *her*. He looked into her bottomless violet eyes, and only saw himself reflected in them.

"I can't leave Earth," she said.

Reid brushed the tip of his nose against hers. "You can."

"I'll never be allowed to." Her voice was sad.

"You will."

Clara turned her face and looked out the musty window and he slid his fingers over her damp cheek, over the bridge of her ear, slipping his fingers into her hair and cupping her head. Her hair fell in waves from its band.

"Do you have a spaceship?"

"I do," he said. She glanced back at him, eyes alight.

"You do?"

Reid chuckled. "A damn decent one too. What kind of Cyborg would I be if I didn't have my own ship?"

She sniffled but laughed with him. "A normal one? Making a normal living wage? One who apparently wasn't ungodly rich and can afford his own spacecraft!"

"Yeah, well, this doctor knows how to doctor anything. Even getting a pregnant female off Earth."

Clara sobered again at his words. "Even so. I wouldn't be able to leave without processing. I've looked into it... a lot, and even if we were—" Her lips went thin.

"Married?" he finished.

"Yes. That. It wouldn't happen. I don't know about being with a Cyborg, but," she placed her hand on her stomach, "there's no way in hell I'd be allowed to leave. Even if I wanted to. And what about Bengie and the bar?"

"Clara, I think you're lying through your teeth."

She shifted on his lap and rolled her eyes. The smell of her berries mixed with the salty tang of her dried tears, and the fading aroma of liquor, had him running his free hand up her leg and under her long skirt to settle over her thigh.

She shivered but didn't stop him, sighing, "If you take me, we'll never be able to return."

Sure we could. But he didn't say it.

"I've always wanted to see what else was out there," she continued. "Do you think it'd be okay? For the babies?"

He bit back a laugh and squeezed her leg and pushed back his chair an extra inch. "Seriously?"

"Don't be an asshole. My hormones are all over the place. I don't think I have any more patience left in me for your hot and cold ride."

Reid pulled at her body and shifted her in his lap until she straddled and faced him. His shaft twitched and pressed up to feel her sex, having missed it every second of every day since she left. "I know your hormones are erratic."

Clara gripped his shoulders and dug her nails into him, biting through the expensive fabric. He had never replaced so many suits since she walked into his life. His own fingers grabbed her hips, under her skirt, and pressed her down onto his erection.

"We can leave. Right now." He held her to him, tight and taut. "If you want."

"Right now? This very moment?"

He hissed. "Yes."

She lifted over him and placed a soft kiss on his lips. Reid lost it. In the seconds that followed, he tore at the barriers between them until the heat of her pussy bathed his groin. Without any preparation, he slid his fingers over her wet folds and spread her opening to take him. He banded an arm around her butt, letting her lean back, and forced his way back into her body. Her cunt accepted him reluctantly until he had her seated to the hilt.

Neither of them spoke as he pulled down Clara's shirt and her breasts spilled out the top. Reid leaned back with a heavy, satisfied groan as his woman rode him, and as she loosened up for him, the tension morphed into desperation. When she tired out, he kept her going—taking charge—unable to stop the mesmerizing sight she created above him, or the clawing and kissing chaotic inferno that had caught them.

When she bit down on his neck, he came, his release guttural and long-awaited as her sheath squeezed him for all he had.

Reid pressed her back onto the rickety table and pulled out, taking in her disheveled state before he dove forward and sucked on her clit. He pulled her shirt up so he could see her scars as he reclaimed her.

Clara writhed her hips and he stopped her. "Stay. Still." Not only because he wanted her to, but because he was unsure of the integrity of the table.

She moaned but settled and he slipped his fingers in and found her g-spot, coaxing her into a heat, into a firestorm. He poured his soul into it, wanting her to know it was a promise for so much more to come.

"Now," he bit out. His fingers went into a frenzy inside her as his mouth latched back onto her bud. She screamed and seized and with a flood of heat, climaxed all over his hand and chin. Reid lapped it up, licked his hand, watching her as she came down, her eyes locked with his.

He helped her up, settling her skirt and pulling up his pants.

Clara eyed him warily. "You really like to embarrass me."

"Wrong." He moved to the wheel and started up the trailer. "I *love* to embarrass you."

Epilogue

• • • •

H e drove them to his flyer stationed several miles away. Afterward, he helped Clara pack her things and load them into his vehicle. Like him, she had very little. It didn't bother him because he knew once they left Earth, they'd collect things together and start a new life elsewhere.

Once they ditched the trailer, he flew them to the largest port in New America, and where his ship was stationed and ready for departure. Clara kept close on his heels as they passed different measures of security and he wrapped a protective arm around her shoulders.

"Don't worry."

"That's easier said than done. I don't want us to get caught."

"There's nothing they can do to stop us." And to prove his point, he led her straight to the entrance of his ship and helped her inside. People looked on, curiously, but no one stepped forward. No one wanted to against a Cyborg. Like a lazy mob mentality, he knew they assumed he had jurisdiction over them. The door shut behind them with a finalizing thud.

He led her to his room to shower and clean up as he made his final preparations. Technology came to life around him and his past-life was on the brink of closure.

I may be the last fucking Cyborg on Earth.

When she was done washing, he knew, and retrieved her from their quarters. Every fiber of her body was tense with fear.

Reid cupped her face and rested his forehead against hers. "The first time is always scary."

155

"Is it?" Clara whined.

"Even for a Cyborg, Clara, and our first time, we had to pilot. The scientists assumed we knew what we were doing, but it was all new on our part."

"Hah. I'd like to have seen that." She smiled and he led her to the bridge, and further into his territory. It thrilled him to know—once they were spaceborne—there would be no way for her to leave it. He'd always be able to keep her safe.

"Ready?"

Clara clapped her hands. "Ready!"

They buckled in and he nuzzled the soft skin of her neck. She still smelled of fear and berries, but he now smelled excitement on her too.

No one stopped him when he requested for take-off. No one stopped them when his ship's thrusters powered on. No one came after them when they shot up into the air and left Earth's atmosphere.

They left the old world behind, the secrets, and the misunderstandings; he didn't look out at the stars in front of him, and he didn't look back at his mistakes. He looked at Clara, at her awestruck face, and her wide eyes seeing the universe for the first time.

He saw it all through her.

Reid coughed, cracked his neck, and loosened his collar. His heart painfully full.

And with giddy laughter filling his ears, he warped them away.

• • • •

"PUSH!" ROSE CAGLEY screeched between Katalina's legs. Clara flinched; in fact, they all did as the female Cyborg forgot how loud her audio tech could go. She sat at Katalina's side and gripped her hand. They held onto each other like it was the end of Ghost itself and that any moment, they'd be consumed by an explosion.

Reid stormed back through the medical door, disheveled, his eyes wide. He left immaculate but had come back looking like he'd just been in a brawl. Minutes earlier he had forcibly dragged Dommik out of the room, eight giant metal limbs and all.

Clara bit down on her tongue and focused back on Katalina, who, despite the chaos, looked the most put together.

Why am I envying her right now? It's not like she was looking forward to giving birth, not after everything she'd seen her friend go through.

Reid waved a scanner over Kat's stomach as another contraction hit her.

"The baby doesn't want to come out," he yelled at Rose.

"I don't give a crap what the baby wants, push, dammit!"

Kat laughed and then her features wrenched. Clara squeezed her hand.

"You're crowning, sweetheart, keep fighting her," Rose pleaded and continued. "Don't give up!"

The sweat poured off Kat and Clara wiped the girl's brow. Their eyes met before another contraction hit. A screaming groan and a heavy breath later and progress was made.

"She's like her daddy, likes the dark."

Several minutes later and the baby girl was out, out, healthy, cleaned up and in Kat's arms. Clara got her hand back, unsure if it was broken until she shook it. When the numbness went away, she was relieved

Reid and Rose had set to work cleaning up the bedding and the room, and after what seemed like days of labor, everything was over. Suddenly it was quiet where it had been loud for so long.

Marcy, Rose's daughter, sat on the other side of Kat and cooed down at the baby. Besides Rose and Marcy, Katalina and Clara were the only women on Ghost. At first, it made her nervous, but then as time went by, she realized that just like on Earth, Ghost held up to its name. The Cyborg city was quiet and had few beings that lived on it, and the rest of its populace were Borgs that came and went as they pleased.

"Do you have a name for her?" Marcy asked, and was the first to break the silence.

"No," Kat whispered, staring at her baby lovingly, as her baby stared back.

"Can't decide?"

She shook her head. "It's not that. I want her to choose her own name. Cyborgs get to choose their name."

"Hmm..."

Clara continued to watch Kat and her child, finding the interaction pleasant but chilling. The baby squirmed and sputtered. No one had any idea how the child was going to react, how it was going to be, and all their speculation was for naught since the little girl appeared and acted human. *Acted.* It was what made her wary.

"You're next, Clara."

She jerked when Reid's voice sounded behind her. His hand covered her shoulder. Clara quickly said her goodbyes and wished Kat and the baby a good first night and left with him. The hallways of Ghost were empty as they made their way from medical.

"Where's Dommik?"

"In quarantine."

"Really? Even now?"

"Even now..." He stopped them and lifted a finger to trace her lips. "They need rest. And he needs to let his systems cool off."

Clara humphed and glanced back from where they came. "Will you react the same way?"

His fingers left her face to thread through her hair and tugged. He was always touching her now and she'd grown used to it.

"No."

"Good. Because you need to be there when it happens. After what I just saw..." she shivered, "I'm going to be scared out of my mind."

"Guess you should've thought about that before you walked into my facility," Reid teased her, his hand moving down her neck, squeezing it.

"I had more important things on my mind."

She smiled and he leaned down to kiss her.

"Me too."

Author's note

· · · ·

Thank you for reading *Mutt*, my surprise Cyborg Shifters novella. If you liked the story or have a comment please leave me a review! I love hearing from fans. You guys keep me going!

I'm currently working on Gunner's book and it's still expected to come Spring 2018.

If you love cyborgs, aliens, anti-heroes, and adventure, follow me onfacebook[1] or through myblog[2] online for information on new releases and updates.

Join mynewsletter[3] for the same information.

Keep an eye out for Gunner's story and BOOK five of Cyborg Shifters and for *Radiant*, an alien reverse harem romance. Turn the page *Radiant*'s blurb...

---

1.   https://www.facebook.com/NaomiLucasRomance/

2.   https://naomilucasauthor.com/

3.   https://app.mailerlite.com/webforms/landing/j1n6p0

Yahiro never thought she would end up in prison. Let alone on a prison ship where escape was impossible. But none of that mattered anymore because while she was curled up in the corner of her cell, the lights went out.

And when they turned back on it was worse.

Ending up on a planet—one so different than Earth—greeted by the screams of those who were injured in the crash and the corpses of those who didn't make it, she sets off with the survivors in hopes of finding a way home.

What she finds instead are three golden aliens that won't let her out of their sight, a city on the back of a giant beast, and a ghost world that will never let her leave.

Coming February 2018...

A reverse harem alien romance.

45007986R00096

Printed in Poland
by Amazon Fulfillment
Poland Sp. z o.o., Wrocław